Doctors Huw and Zara Morgan are on holiday on the Solway Firth when they become aware of IRA weapons and explosives being smuggled ashore. Having, in their younger days, been involved in intelligence work for the British Secret Service, they decide to investigate. They are captured by the smugglers and imprisoned in a disused ice-house on the shore.

Physical escape being impossible, Huw seeks relief from his from his immediate discomfort by recalling the circumstances in which he met Zara during the latter days of World War 2. Back then, as a young Naval Officer in the Special Boat Squadron, he had penetrated the Scheldt Estuary to gather intelligence about the mine-fields and other defences that the Allies would have to overcome if they were to be able to open up the port of Antwerp. His work there culminated in the Allied bombing and invasion of the Island of Walcheron, an important but little known aspect of the liberation of Europe.

Whilst on this mission, Huw was in radio contact with his controller in Britain. They arranged to meet, neither knowing anything about the other. The controller turned out to be an Indian girl named Zara. They met, fell in love and married. Eventually, they both qualified as doctors, she a surgeon, he a GP.

In civilian life, they continued to communicate secretly with one another by Morse code, a talent that they were able to put to good use in the years they worked in Northern Ireland, gathering intelligence for the anti-terrorist forces whilst patching up wounded IRA men.

Now, in the latter days of their lives, the opportunity to serve their country again presents itself and they eventually are able to frustrate the IRA plan to bring a fresh bombing campaign to the streets of London.

HEROIC HEARTS

A NOVEL BY
Webster Simpson

ISBN 0 9538690-3-2

Published by
Itelsor Ltd
Trendell House
3 Lintrathen Street, Dundee DD5 8EF
Tel: 01382 825629 Fax: 01382 832316

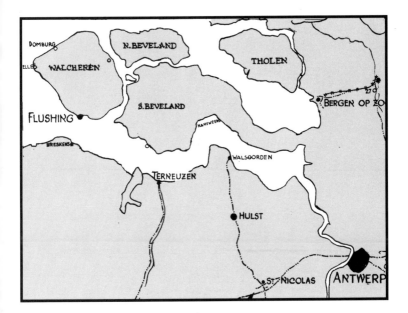

Chapter 1

Scotland - West Coast-Autumn 1996

Huw Morgan painfully regained consciousness. How long he had been out, he had no way of knowing. His head was splitting. His legs ached with cramp. The gag over his mouth made breathing difficult. He struggled to look round him, but, with his feet tied together and his hands tightly bound behind his back, any movement was a terrible effort. He was in utter darkness, lying on a flag-stone floor and breathing air polluted by a foul mixture of stale sea-weed and rotting fish. He was shivering convulsively. Huw had not been a doctor for over forty years without knowing that this was caused only partly by cold. Being banged on the head and knocked unconscious is not good for anyone. For a frail man of eighty-two with a serious heart condition, it was a wonder he was only suffering from shock. Such an experience could easily have been fatal.

Huw forced himself to think back over the

circumstances that had placed him in his present position. Pride! That was his weakness. That was what lay behind the series of events that had brought him here. Zara had been right. It had been foolish to go ahead alone. They should have waited for back-up. At least Zara must have escaped. Whether she knew where he was imprisoned and whether she could bring help in time, he had no way of telling. Everything depended on Zara, wherever she was.

Never mind where Zara was. Where was he? He knew where he had been before he had been struck down from behind. He had been on the fore-shore, not far from Castle Stalker, on Loch Linnhe. Ever since their honeymoon in the Spring of 1946, Zara and he had been coming back regularly to Oban for holidays. Although neither had said anything, both knew this would be the last time. Whether Zara's cancer would carry her off before Huw's heart finally packed up, neither of them knew, despite their impressive collective medical knowledge. Huw might go at any time, at least with merciful abruptness. Both knew that Zara's inoperable cancer would soon cause pain that could not be controlled outside a hospital. They had struggled to make it here for their 50th wedding anniversary. Both of them knew it would be their last together. There was little realistic chance of their being able to come back to

Oban for their 51st next Spring, so they had come in Autumn instead. Even if they did have the 51st anniversary together, both knew that neither of them was likely to be alive when the 52nd came round.

It was there, at the Royal Hotel just after lunch, as he waited in the foyer for Zara, that Huw had overheard the telephone conversation. Had it been in English, he would have politely moved out of ear-shot. However, it was now nearly twenty years since he heard anyone converse in Irish Gaelic and, inevitably, his curiosity had been aroused. This was one of several languages he had a good grasp of. He turned and looked at the man making the call. Quickly he swung his head back and tried to look absolutely absorbed in the newspapers on the rack in front of him. Brendan McPhee! It was nearly a quarter of a century since he had last seen him. What was he doing in the Royal? Huw tried unsuccessfully to eavesdrop but did not catch enough to make coherent sense of the conversation. He did not dare close the gap between them, although there was little risk of McPhee recognising him. After all, the first time they had met, McPhee had been unconscious most of the time as Zara had extracted the bullet from his thigh and, together, the husband and wife team of GP and surgeon, had set the IRA man's smashed leg. It was madness to do such a complex piece of surgery in the insanitary environment of an isolated Ulster farmhouse, but McPhee would not hear of being taken to hospital. Neither doctor wanted to operate. What would the British Medical Association say about such proceedings? What would the British Government say? But neither the BMA nor Her Majesty's Government was standing behind the husband and wife team with a sub-machine gun. So the two had operated, and the presence of the veteran IRA man making a phone call in Gaelic in an Oban hotel over twenty years later was eloquent testimony to a combination of skill and good fortune.

In the years that followed, the Morgans had met McPhee several times. He had been fulsome in his praise of the two doctors and had taken personal pride in promoting their skills among other IRA casualties of the Ulster 'Troubles'. On a further three occasions McPhee himself had required patching up, but never for anything very serious. The years that had elapsed since the last of these had so changed the appearance of the ageing doctors that it was indeed unlikely that McPhee would notice them. However, thought Huw, better safe than sorry.

Zara appeared a minute or two later. Huw hurried her out of the hotel. His caution was probably unnecessary. Huw would find it hard to admit, but twenty years and rampant cancer had changed his Zara beyond recognition. Gone was her raven-black hair. The side effects of chemotherapy had seen to that. Zara now wore a grey wig that was not inappropriate for a woman in her late seventies. It did, however, accentuate her dark complexion. She had never been over-weight, and the loss of two and a half stone had reduced her to a pathetically frail state. However, Huw was taking no chances. Their survival to a ripe old age had been due to such a cautious attitude and old habits die hard. Once well clear of the hotel, Huw explained.

"I've just seen an old patient of yours. Brendan McPhee! You remember!"

Remember! How could she ever forget! That cold December night in 1972 when the door-bell rang just after mid-night. Three masked and armed men outside. There was no question of the two doctors being given the option of whether they wished to help or not. At gun-point they had been bundled into the back of a tired old van and driven for what had seemed hours, but in fact was less than two. The first intimation that their journey was nearly over came when the van pitched and tossed its way up a deeply rutted farm-track, eventually coming to a halt outside a nearly derelict house. The two were roughly ordered out and pushed into the large farm kitchen. There, on a couch lay a man in his early twenties, his leg swathed in blood-soaked bandages. He was sweating profusely and showed all the classic signs of a man in deep traumatic shock.

A brief examination told both doctors that this was a near-hopeless case. In hospital, with a first-class theatre and a skilled team, coupled with excellent intensive-care facilities, it might be possible to do something, but an emergency operation here was almost bound to be fatal. They had only the most basic equipment with them. No one in his right mind would undertake surgery like this without administering a general anaesthetic. However, faced with the determination of their captors and, more particularly, with the simple eloquence of their guns, the doctors operated. The first thing was to prepare the primitive facilities. The two doctors issued orders which, to their surprise, were instantly obeyed. The kitchen table was scrubbed again and again with disinfectant. The fire was stoked until the temperature in the stuffy room was nearly unbearably hot. All unnecessary furniture was removed and every available light in the house was rigged up to improve the pathetic standard of illumination.

Despite this, the Morgans were filled with despair. There was simply no back-up, no skilled theatre nursing staff, no anaesthetist, virtually no equipment. Sterilising had to be done by boiling all instruments and dressings in a cooking pot on the coal-fired range. The chances of the patient dying on the table seemed overwhelming. Then what would be their fate? However, there was nothing else for it so they got on with the job.

It was a long and complicated operation and both marvelled that the patient's heart stood the shock. Amazingly, there was no secondary infection to complicate what was already an intricate enough procedure and the patient recovered in as short a time as might have been hoped for in a first-class hospital. Dr Huw and Dr Zara Morgan were frankly amazed, but wisely kept their feelings to themselves.

That was only the beginning. Over the next seven years, there were many such clandestine operations. All their efforts to persuade the terrorists to set up a reasonably modern clinic were fruitless. Obsessed with security, the IRA men seldom took the Morgans to the same place twice. The result was that, every time without fail, valuable time had to be spent trying to produce a tolerably sterile environment. Not all their operations had a successful outcome, a fact that did not surprise the Morgans. However, the inevitable failures were accepted philosophically enough by the IRA. It was indeed surprising that the success rate was as high as it was considering how tired the doctors often were. The

GP's surgery in central Belfast was busy enough with more orthodox patients and Zara's duties as an orthopaedic surgeon in the hospital were demanding in the extreme. The strain of being called out, sometimes to work all night on IRA casualties, was a nearly intolerable burden. However, through time, the two doctors had won the confidence of the terrorists and in due course had become a very important source of intelligence for the British security services.

"McPhee! Are you sure? Whatever is he doing here?" demanded Zara.

"It was him all right. You must have done a marvellous job! If you weren't looking for it, I'll swear you'd never notice the limp. If he'd been taken to hospital, I'm sure they would have amputated. You're brilliant! But I always knew that!"

"Seriously, though. What's he up to? I'm sure he's not just here for the scenery. It grieves me to think that we patched him up so he could carry on his career of mayhem. I can't imagine a man like that retiring, so what's his game now?"

"I don't know. Perhaps even terrorists need a holiday now and then! After all, shooting people and blowing things up must be rather hard on the nerves! A man needs a break from work. As a doctor, you should know that," said Huw teasingly.

"Come off it! If he's here, you can be sure he's up to no good."

"I tried to hear what he was saying but he was just too far away. All I got was that he would phone again tonight. Perhaps we can get closer and eavesdrop more successfully."

"Perhaps we should tell the police."

"Tell them what? We've absolutely no concrete evidence to give them. We happen to know that this man is an IRA terrorist and that he's staying as a guest in this hotel. But how can we hope to persuade the police? We can't even substantiate our allegations about him, let alone prove he's up to mischief here. Who's going to pay any attention to us?"

"You're right, Huw, as usual. Unless we can get a bit more to go on, there's really nothing we can do. I suppose we can keep an eye on him, but that's about all."

"Let's get the car and sit out a little along from the hotel. If he comes out, we can follow at a discreet distance and see what happens."

"Sounds daft to me, but I'll go along with it. You get the car and I'll get myself ready."

Huw drove the car a hundred yards or so past the hotel and the two settled down to watch. They did not have to wait long. McPhee, accompanied by a younger man, emerged and crossed the car park to a small estate car. Minutes later, the two cars left Oban heading northwards. The afternoon traffic was light so Huw let a car and a motor cycle overtake to make sure that he was not immediately behind the other vehicle. At an unhurried pace, they went northwards across the bridge at Connel.

"They could be going anywhere," remarked Zara. "Fort William. Inverness even."

"Somehow I don't think so. They would have left earlier in the day if they were going a long way. Their speed suggests they are not going very far. We'll tail them for a few more miles. If it does look like they're leaving the area, we can give up then."

There were few side-turnings so Huw was able to follow at a considerable distance, usually with two or three other vehicles between him and the McPhee car. At the village of Portnacroish, the estate car stopped. Huw drove on past and turned into a side street. Zara and he slipped out of the car and walked back to the main road in time to see McPhee and his companion emerge from the village post office. The Irishman turned his car and set off southwards. For a moment the Morgans thought they had lost the scent, but the estate car took the very narrow road to the right sign-posted Port Appin.

"I don't think we need keep them in sight," said Huw after the two had hurriedly set out in their own car along the same road. "From the map it looks as though they can only be going to Port Appin, although I notice there's a ferry from there to the island off-shore."

They drove down the short distance to Port Appin which turned out to be a mere handful of houses on the loch-side. McPhee's car was parked outside the village shop so, following a sign marked 'Ferry', Huw drove passed and parked in a car-park some fifty yards farther on at the point where the road ended.

"Now what?" asked Zara.

"We watch. If we go one at a time, he's less likely to spot that he's being followed. Put on your dark glasses and take the binoculars. I'll do likewise but have the camera. With a bit of luck, we can keep a discreet watch without being noticed."

So the two left the car and, for the next two hours or more, seemed totally preoccupied with the bird life on the shore and the scenery around them. The two Irishmen also appeared very interested in ornithology and walked along the shore as the tide receded. By late afternoon it was well out and McPhee and his friend, now half a mile from the village, picked their way out on a hard stretch of sand between the mud-flats completely oblivious to the fact that they were being watched every moment.

Eventually, having presumably seen all they wanted to, the two men went back to their car. Huw and Zara watched it leave.

"I think we can safely assume they're headed back to the hotel. There's no need for us to follow closely. No point in risking being spotted at this stage. The question is what do we do now?" said Huw.

"We've still absolutely nothing to go on. Certainly there's nothing we can take to the police.

"The only thing we can do is to keep our eyes and ears open and hope that, if there's something going on, we can get a clue as to what it is. Meanwhile, let's get back to Oban or we'll miss dinner and that really will be serious!"

After dinner that evening, Huw seated himself close to the pay-phone McPhee had used last time. It seemed likely that the Irishman would use it rather than a mobile or the phone in his room, either of which might conceivably be trace back to him. Sure enough, from behind his newspaper, Huw saw McPhee come to the phone just before ten o'clock. Very discreetly he listened.

"High tide tomorrow's about 11p.m. Drop the stuff over the side as soon as there's sufficient water. You'll be able to lie off Castle Stalker without anyone paying any attention to you. Make sure you're bang on...." Then followed a complex series of numerals that might have made sense to someone with a Global Positioning Device but to Huw it meant nothing.

"Make sure you use your GPS and get it right. There's a hard ridge of sand out through the mud-flats. We'll pick the stuff up as the tide ebbs. By daylight, it'll all be on the van and no-one will even know we've been there."

Huw got up and moved away before his presence was noticed. From a safe distance, he watched McPhee walk away. If one was looking for it, a slight limp could just be discerned. Huw could not help feeling proud of his wife's professional skill. In the finest operating theatre in the land, no-one would have given much for the chances of Brendan McPhee surviving that first bullet wound without an amputation. Yet here he was, with scarcely a limp, following an operation on the kitchen table of a remote farm-house with only the barest of amenities. The devil certainly looked after his own!

Back in their room, he reported back to Zara

"I was eavesdropping when he was on the phone. He's arranged to pick something up on the mud-flats tomorrow night. He was talking in Gaelic again. It was obviously to someone who has a boat. He gave a map-reference and he's expecting delivery tomorrow. He did mention Castle Stalker so it must be up near Port Appin right enough. I suggest we set ourselves up down by Castle Stalker tomorrow evening. He said high-tide is about eleven. My guess is that the boat, whatever it is, will come in close some time between ten and mid-night, probably pretending to be simply anchoring for the night in a sheltered spot. At the appropriate spot, the cargo will be dropped over the side. Then McPhee will pick it up as the tide ebbs, probably about 3am."

"What do you think they're landing?" asked Zara.

"Guns or explosives would be my guess. It's obviously something they don't care to bring across by ferry. The one thing you can be sure of is that McPhee's up to no good!"

"Could it be drugs?"

"Possibly. A lot of the IRA funds come from drug-peddling, but, as far as I know, they concentrate on the Irish market - both north and south. I don't think they're likely to be bringing drugs to mainland Britain, but you never know!"

"Shouldn't we get the police now? We've a bit more to go on at least. They would have the resources to watch the whole coast-line. Besides, if it's what you think, it could get dangerous."

"I can't see the local bobbies paying much attention to a couple of geriatrics. Apart from that, even if we did convince them, the first thing they would do would be to tell us to keep out of it. If there's excitement to be had, I want to be in the middle of it, not pushed to one side. It's a pity there's no-one left from the old days who we could phone. The trouble is, we've outlived them all. The last to go was Robertson and it must be ten years since he died. Now there's no one left who would remember us. No! Let's trail them ourselves and, when we've got something concrete to report, we'll call out the cavalry. Besides, it'll be like old times. Life gets rather flat at times. We could both do with a bit of excitement, don't you think? We might yet do something really useful. I don't want to 'rust unburnished but to shine in use!'"

"You love quoting Tennyson's 'Ulysses', don't you?" Zara grinned. "At least you didn't throw in the bit about being 'matched with an aged wife!'"

"No, but I did think about saying 'some work of

noble note may yet be done!' Seriously, I'd like one more adventure and, if one gets handed to us on a plate, I think we should take it."

"It's those mud-flats up by Castle Stalker!" Zara exclaimed. "You're hankering after your lost youth on the River Scheldt! OK. I'll go along with your madness one more time. We'll have the mobile phone with us so we can get the police on the job as soon as we're sure that the cargo is arms or explosives."

"Right! We'll run up to Portnacroish again tomorrow. It'll be important to really see the lie of the land. Even now, I think we can make an intelligent guess as to where they'll bring the stuff ashore. Tomorrow we can position ourselves discreetly to see what's going on and act accordingly."

- - - - - - - -

The next day, having told the hotel manager they would not be back for dinner, the elderly couple drove out on the road past Connel and Loch Creran back to the tiny village of Port Appin. The sleepy cluster of houses by the shore seemed once again largely deserted, although there were one or two people chatting outside the village shop. The Morgans left their car at the surprisingly large car-park that looked much to big for such a small place. Most of the cars in it no doubt belonged to ornithologists and others who had taken the little ferry across to the near-by island of Lismore. Huw parked and the pair walked back to the shop. Here, Zara went in, leaving Huw seated on an up-turned boat drawing thoughtfully on his pipe as he watched a couple of teenage lads canoeing in the bay. He was still sitting there when Zara returned.

"Day-dreaming, are you?" she said with a grin.

"Takes me back," replied her husband, as he watched the boys bring their craft into land farther along the shore.

They strolled along to where the two lads were hauling their little crafts up the beach, turning them upside-down and stowing the paddles under them.

"Hmm! Might be useful, that. If the Irish boat tonight is lying off one of those skerries out there, I could borrow a canoe and sneak a look at them."

"Be your age, Huw! When were you last in a canoe? What we're thinking about doing is mad enough without you trying to drown yourself!"

"Canoeing's like riding a bike. You don't forget. I know I can't paddle the way I once did, but I could still show those kids a thing or two!"

"Well, never mind dreaming about that. What's

the plan of campaign for tonight?"

"Simple! We leave the car in the car-park, come through the village and sit on that knoll up there. We'll have a commanding view of the whole bay, unless, as I say, the boat lies hidden beyond one of those small islands. Whatever happens, they'll have to carry the cargo up to the road at some quiet spot and load it on a vehicle so we should be able to see them."

Zara looked out to where he was pointing. In the foreground was the narrow road round the bay with a strip of grass interspersed with bushes between it and the shore itself. The tide was well out, exposing sand and mud for fifty yards or more. Then, a hundred yards of water separated the mud from the first of the skerries, low-lying reefs of rock, some covered with seaweed which doubtless were below water at high tide and others, slightly higher, with a thin covering of grass and heather clinging to the crest of them. Beyond these reefs was deeper water and beyond that the small island on which the imposing mass of Castle Stalker was built. The castle itself was at one and the same time impressive and foreboding. As she looked at it, Zara shivered involuntarily.

"They'll be taking a bit of a risk loading a van in the small hours of the morning, Huw. Anyone who sees them will guess something fishy is going on and is likely to call the police."

"Right enough! Perhaps that's why McPhee was telling his accomplice to drop the stuff over the side. I think they'll come on foot at low tide in the early hours of the morning. Then they'll be able to carry it ashore and hide it among the gorse bushes. That way they'll be able to pick it up quietly in day-time and not attract any attention."

"Perhaps we'd better get back to the car. It's just possible that McPhee'll be back here reconnoitring and it would be somewhat embarrassing if we bumped into him!"

"Yes. We'd better keep out of the way. Let's go somewhere north of here and find a place to eat. That way there'll be no risk of meeting him and we can easily be back in good time for this evening. Perhaps I'm worrying needlessly, however. It would be surprising if he recognised us after all these years. After all, let's face it. We've both changed since the last time we saw him."

Chapter 2

Dressed in dark, warm clothes, the two returned to Port Appin later that evening. The car-park was nearly empty and there was certainly no sign of any van that might be suitable for carrying whatever the cargo might be.

"It's always possible that it's not anything as bulky as guns and explosives. Maybe they are into smuggling drugs to fund the IRA work in Ulster," said Zara. "That way, they wouldn't need a van. The stuff would be small enough to go in his estate car."

"That's possible, I suppose. But somehow I still don't think it'll be drugs. Besides, I'm sure he said something about a van. Weapons and bombs are much more McPhee's line of business. He's a dedicated terrorist and's not likely to stoop to assisting mere fund-raising activities. Apart from which I really am sure that McPhee specifically mentioned a van. Come on. We'll get ourselves established up among those bushes. I'll bring a rug in case its a long wait."

It was a long wait. Darkness closed in around

them, an oppressive darkness broken only by the lights of infrequent cars on the road below and the regular flashing of a navigation buoy far out in the firth. About ten, Huw sensed, rather than saw, a boat carrying no lights slipping noiselessly through the water half a mile or so off shore. He peered through the deep gloom but could make out nothing.

"I think they're the other side of the bay," he whispered. "The boat must be hidden behind one of the islands. Look! I'm going to borrow a canoe and slip out to the lee of Castle Stalker. I should be able to see without being seen. You go and get the car. Drive round the bay and leave it half a mile or more up the road. When I'm sure of what's going on, I'll make a landing on the far shore."

"You're mad! How do you think we're we going to meet up in the dark?"

"Easy! I'll give an owl-hoot. The letter 'Z'. You reply with 'H'. There's no way anyone's going to notice that an owl happens to be using Morse!"

The couple slid down the bank to the road. With some difficulty, Huw found the canoes. With much more difficulty, he rolled one over and launched it. The cold water nearly took his breath away as he waded out ankle deep and climbed into it. However, the years seemed to slip off him as he noiselessly paddled the light craft out into the bay. Meanwhile Zara, stiff from sitting in the damp night air, made her best speed to the car-park. By the time she returned to Huw's launching point there was no sign of him.

His eyes well adjusted to the dark, Huw could just make out the distant looming mass of Castle Stalker, standing as it does on an off-shore rock. Soon he reached the first of the skerries and cautiously steered round it. Ahead there was a slight scuffling sound and the occasional splash near the shore on the north side of the bay. Lying low in the canoe, he paddled the craft silently through the water so slowly as not to make a ripple. The furtive noises increased as he drew nearer. Then he saw the dim shape of a fishing boat, its bows pointing out to the open water of the firth. Whatever activity was going on was at the stern. With great care, Huw dipped his paddle and manoeuvred the canoe towards a reef that barely broke the surface some eighty yards away. In the shelter of it, he crouched down and waited as the unloading of the boat proceeded.

After what seemed an eternity, there came the dull rumble of the diesel engine being started and the clank of an anchor being cautiously raised. Still with no lights, the fishing boat slowly and almost noiselessly put to sea, passing within fifty yards of where Huw was. Then there was utter silence.

After some minutes, Huw eased the canoe round and, still very cautiously, headed for the northern shore. He slipped past the westmost point of the headland and made a landing on a sandy beach. Pausing long enough to pull the craft ashore, he eased himself into the scrub that lined the shore. There, he pulled off his shoes and wrung what water he could from his sodden socks. The silence was complete. Standing up unsteadily on his numb feet, he stumbled up the beach into the scrub. With great care, he worked his way through the gorse and juniper until he came to a track which obviously led up to the public road. To one side was the arched entrance to what he recognised as an old ice-house. Beside it lay the mouldering hulks of a couple of small fishing boats. Crouching in the deep darkness between them, he gave a gentle owl-hoot.

"Toooot. Toooot. Toot. Toot." Pause. "Toooot. Toooot. Toot. Toot." Two dashes and two dots : the letter 'Z'.

Out of the darkness some distance to the north came an answering call. "Toot. Toot. Toot. Toot." four dots - the letter 'H'.

As quietly as he could, Huw slipped out from the

cover of the boats and crept up the path. A hundred yards or so on, he tooted gently once more. This time the reply was very close and a few moments later he could just make out Zara's thin shape against the dark grey track.

"Thank goodness you're safe!" she whispered. "I had visions of you being run down by that boat. You'd only last a few minutes in that water."

"Well, I'm here safe and sound," Huw replied, trying not to shiver as he spoke. The feeling was slowly and painfully returning to his feet. "We'd better not linger on this track. McPhee and company could turn up at any moment." So saying, he drew his wife in among the scrub that pervaded the whole area.

"Do we phone the police now?" asked Zara.

"Not yet, I don't think. We've still practically nothing to go on. I think we'll have to wait for the tide to go out and then make sure that something was dropped overboard. Come on. We'll get back to the shore and hide in the bushes until we see what happens next."

They selected a dense clump of juniper some distance from where the boat had been anchored.

"We'll see well enough from here. Anyone coming to the beach here has to pass within five yards of us so we'll definitely not miss them." Huw said, and the two huddled close together to share their warmth in the pre-dawn chill.

For nearly two hours nothing stirred. Huw struggled to stay awake, while Zara shivered with cold. Suddenly she tensed and squeezed her husband's hand. Huw strained his ears. Someone was approaching with evident caution. The two held their breath as two dark figures stole by, passing noiselessly almost like ghosts down the track and on to the shore. It was still much too dark to see who they were or what they were doing. Huw leaned over and whispered in Zara's ear.

"You move back and hide somewhere near that ice-house. I'm going to creep nearer. If they are bringing the stuff ashore, I'll try to make sure it's what we think it is. When I am sure, I'll hoot. "Yes" and you can phone the police. Make sure you're far enough away for the bandits to have no chance of hearing your voice."

"What if they catch you?"

"I don't intend to let them, but, if they do, I'll yell and you can phone for help."

Slowly and carefully, the two crept off in opposite directions. Keeping just to the landward side of the track, Huw crawled very slowly to where he could hear the scrunch of footsteps on the gravelly shore. In the darkness he could just make out the two men struggling up the beach carrying a heavy drum between them. They dumped it down among the gorse beside the track and went back down on to the mud-flats. Huw eased himself a little nearer and, at the same time, started counting the seconds. It was fully two hundred seconds before the men returned, again with a drum. As soon as they had put it down and withdrawn, Huw, still counting, crept over to it. His hands were quite numb and it was with some difficulty that he unscrewed the bung at the top of the plastic drum. Inside was a grey powder. He sniffed and smelled a slight ammonia sort of odour. All the time he was counting. In good time, he replaced the bung and withdrew into the shelter of the gorse again. A few seconds later he heard the heavy breathing of the two men as they struggled up the beach, this time carrying a heavy long wooden box.

Once they had again moved off down the beach, Huw eased himself out of cover. Part of him wanted to give the owl-hoot signal there and then, but another part wanted to know what this crate contained. He bent over it, taking in the fact that it was tightly closed and coated with some kind of water-proof finish. From behind him came a slight sound and he swung round just in time to see a heavy stick descending on his head, but too late to avoid it. Then everything went black.

- - - - - - -

That was how Huw came to be where he was. Cursing his own stupidity under his breath, he wriggled impotently. The ropes were cutting into his wrists. Lying still, his body ached and cramp set in in his leg. Any attempt at movement brought stabbing pains from his bonds and an alarming tightness in his chest. The darkness was intense. The silence was oppressive. There was nothing to do but wait. Huw wondered where Zara was. He detached himself from his present plight by thinking back on the unusual set of circumstances that had brought them together all those years ago. As he lay in the darkness, he drifted back fifty and more years to another time and another place where he had lain shivering in the dark.

Chapter 3

Autumn 1944 on the Estuary of the River Scheldt

Lieutenant Huw Morgan lay huddled in his sleeping bag, shivering convulsively. The conflict in Europe was now in its sixth and final year. The tide of war had at last turned in the Allies' favour. The Normandy D-Day invasion had succeeded and the Nazi forces were slowly being pushed back across France and the Low Countries. The Russian Army was advancing equally slowly and at even more appalling cost in the east. However, though the eventual outcome of the war was no longer in doubt, long months of struggle, hardship and bloodshed lay ahead before Europe would finally be free.

Too cold to sleep and with gnawing hunger pains, Huw lay uncomfortably in the chain locker of a wrecked barge on the mud-flats of the Scheldt estuary. The barge was one of hundreds that had been commandeered by Hitler in his victorious, heady days of 1940 for his planned invasion of Britain. It had been bombed and sunk by the Royal Air Force as it was being towed to the port of Flushing to be converted to a troop-landing ship. Now, abandoned for four years, only the prow stuck out of the water at high tide. At low tide most of the hull was exposed, but the craft was completely inaccessible on foot across the treacherous mud banks. Below the high-tide mark, the rust on the hull was completely concealed by the dense sea-weed that covered the steel plates. That small part of the hull that was above water had now lost whatever paint it once had and what was not red with rust was white with bird excrement. Drift-wood and reeds accumulated round the hatches of the hold and a decaying corpse, caught by the tattered remains of a military uniform, dangled grotesquely over the port side.

The chain locker, accessible only from under water through a great bomb-hole in the side of the hull, made a safe, though damp and uncomfortable, hiding place. Some light filtered in through the two ports for the anchor chains and also through a crack in the deck some two inches wide and four feet long. As the tide ebbed, fresh air was sucked in through these ports and through the crack. This meant that, although the air in the ten feet by five feet area in the locker became pretty foul at high tide, reeking of guano, at least the cramped four feet high space that had been his living quarters for the past four weeks was fully ventilated twice a day. When the tide ebbed, a gash in the bulkhead which formed the rear wall of the chain-locker exposed the dark, silted-up hold of the barge. Everything was covered in slime and sea-weed and the smell was nauseating. The inside of the chain-locker was only moderately limed with guano but this gave off a strong smell of ammonia. All the steel-work was heavily corroded and rust flaked from the walls and ceiling of Huw's hiding place.

The River Scheldt, a sluggish and heavily polluted water-way in peace-time, was now an open sewer carrying the detritus of major cities upstream such as Antwerp. These cities discharged not only their sewage, but all the flotsam and jetsam of war. More than the one bloated corpse had drifted past the wreck. It would not have been so bad if they drifted past once, but some had revisited the barge on several successive tides as the waters ebbed and flowed.

Huw's work in Holland was over now. His problem was how to get back from this hostile environment to Allied lines. As he lay in the dank darkness, he went over the chain of events that had brought him here. Huw had been born in the Welsh mining village of Cwmparc on the day before the First World War began in 1914. His father, a miner, as, indeed, his father had been before him, was determined his son should not follow him down the pits. With his own lungs permanently damaged by the rigours of deep-mine working, Evan Morgan had had to retire at fifty-four, by which age he had the looks and the manner of a man of seventy. It was, however, one thing to decide that young Huw should not go down the mines, but quite another for gainful employment to be found for him elsewhere. A deep world-wide economic depression meant that there was no real choice in employment. Indeed, a youngster like Huw would be lucky indeed to find any kind of work. The upshot had been a compromise. Huw had undergone intensive training in mine rescue and first aid. He did not regularly go down the pits, but when he did, it was always in the most dangerous circumstances. The first-aid training was a matter of enlightened self-interest on the part of the mining Company. Huw was paid a pittance, but was expected to act as company doctor in all but the most serious of cases, with a consequent substantial saving in medical fees for his bosses. However, it was this aspect of his work that Huw found most fulfilling. He learnt everything he could, scrounging text-books from the friendly local doctor, whilst, at the same time, pestering the kindly old man with incessant questions.

It was when he was sent to Belgium to learn new mine-rescue techniques that he discovered his flair for learning languages. He was there only ten weeks, but returned home to Cwmparc not only with a working knowledge of Flemish, but also reasonably competent in Dutch as well. Of course, that was not why he had been sent to Belgium. He was there to learn to use the latest breathing apparatus. In a round-about way, it was because of that trip to Belgium ten years earlier that Huw now lay shivering in the rust-bucket in the Scheldt.

When war was declared in 1939, Huw had been quick to volunteer. With his experience in the use of breathing apparatus, he was snatched up by the Royal Navy, desperately short of divers as it was. After intensive training, Huw spent much of the first three years of the war employed in diving. Sometimes this meant removing under-water obstructions or repairing damaged ships or dock installations such as dry docks damaged by bombing. Other times it was straightforward salvage work, raising wrecks. Then he had been drafted into the highly secret Special Boat Squadron. Here, his work had been varied. There had been the weeks spent at a top secret location in the Shetland Islands, developing what were to become known as Motor Submersible Canoes. Then there had been the excursions to various beaches along the French coast during the weeks immediately prior to the Allied invasion of Normandy on D-Day. Here, small parties of marines and Special Boat Squadron experts were transferred several miles off the coast into small dories.

These made their way inshore and then a second transfer took place, this time to inflatable boats. The divers went close into the beaches and charted undersea obstacles and anti-landing-craft devices, whilst the marines actually landed and mapped any mine-fields on the beaches themselves.

D-Day plus two saw Huw on the Normandy beaches even though these were still sometimes coming under shell-fire, doing repair work on damaged landing-craft. From there, he was re-assigned to Luma Voe in the Shetlands and back to the Motor Submersible Canoes. There had been significant progress made on these in the few short months he had been away. The Mark 2 craft was a considerable improvement on the earlier experimental boats. It was about fifteen feet long, with a cock-pit for the canoeist near the stern. On the surface it was capable of six miles per hour under power and had a range of some forty miles. Submerged, the speed was nearly halved and the range cut to twelve miles. Despite their small size, the MSCs could cope with five or six foot waves, although, in these conditions, the pilot-swimmer would be much more comfortable running submerged.

Under water, the pilot-swimmer used self-contained breathing apparatus and the boat was driven by a battery-powered electric motor. On the surface, the craft could be paddled just like a conventional canoe, vastly extending its range. The MSC's great advantage was it was so small as to be invisible to radar. It was almost undetectable to sonar when fully submerged and very hard to see with the naked eye, especially if the pilot was running with the hull submerged and only his head above the surface. The pilot, controlled his craft by means of a small joy-stick in the cockpit. Pushing it forward inclined the hydroplanes and took the craft downwards, whilst reversing the movement brought it up. The same joy-stick controlled the rudder. To the pilot's right were the controls for the compressed air and the valves which regulated the MSC's trim. A simple hand-pump enabled the pilot to keep his reserve of compressed air topped up by operating it for a couple of minutes each time he surfaced. Before submerging, the pilot adjusted the water level in buoyancy tanks fore and aft until the boat had neutral buoyancy, floating just below the surface with only his head and shoulders above the water. He then eased the boat ahead on its electric motor. Hydroplanes, controlled by the joy-stick, took it up or down in the water as required. Periodic adjustments to the amount of air in the buoyancy tanks, made by releasing air and letting in more water, or by pressing the valve that squirted in high pressure air to expel some water, enabled the craft to be kept in trim.

Practice enabled Huw to be able to make the MSC to porpoise, so that he could surface with scarcely a ripple, get his bearings, then slip below the surface again. Handling the craft along a coast-line could be tricky. Streams and rivers pouring fresh water into the sea caused the density of the water to vary. A MSC approaching the out-flow from a river would abruptly go down, hitting the sea-bed quite hard if the pilot was not alert. Likewise, it might equally suddenly surface if it ran out of fresh and into salt water. As the anticipated use of MSCs was to penetrate river estuaries and to enter enemy harbours, coping with these varying conditions was going to be vital if MSC and pilot were to survive. None of the team of pilots had been told what the ultimate purpose of the MSCs would be. Training in mock attacks on naval ships in Scapa Flow, which included the placing of limpet mines, supported the commonly held view in the closely-knit circle of pilots that they were to be used against the Tirpitz. That great German battleship was still holed up in a Norwegian Fjord and was a constant threat to Allied Atlantic shipping. Even without actually putting to sea, it menaced the convoys transporting supplies to the Russian allies. Several major British Navy ships had to be perpetually in a state of instant readiness in case the Tirpitz made a foray out of the fiords.

Suddenly in mid-September, Huw had been recalled to London. After a wearisome journey by lorry, then ferry, then railway train, altogether lasting a continuous twenty-six hours he reached London. There he was escorted to a bunker deep under the Admiralty buildings. Alongside others present, he felt positively junior. The meeting was chaired by an Admiral of the Fleet and no-one other than himself seemed to be below the rank of Captain. The army was represented by a Brigadier and the RAF by an Air-Commodore.

"Gentlemen. The subject is Antwerp. We captured Antwerp nearly three weeks ago. On the face of it, this should have been a major step forward. Antwerp was one of the busiest Continental ports before the war. The port installations are relatively intact. It has a dock system and railways that can cope with 100,000 tons a day. Bringing it into use will shorten our supply lines by almost 300 miles. That means cutting the transportation time of supplies by two days and saving tens of thousands of gallons of fuel which we would much rather use in tanks and aircraft than in lorries.

"The snag is, Antwerp is almost 60 miles from the sea. It is reached by sailing up the River Scheldt. The problem is that the Nazis still control both banks. We know that the shipping channel has been mined, but we do not know accurately to what degree. There's a pocket of veteran German troops cut off on the south bank. They're being supplied from the north side and are proving very difficult to move. The Canadian Army's 3rd and 4th Divisions are pressing them hard, but it's taking a terrible time to shift them. On the north side, over thirty heavy guns are firmly emplaced. Any mine-sweeper approaching the mouth of the Scheldt would be blown clean out of the water. The island of Walcheron is on the north side of the estuary at the mouth of the river and it is the key to Antwerp.

"So long as the Nazis hold Walcheron, we can't use Antwerp. It's as simple as that. With the strength of their coastal defences on Walcheron, any sea-borne invasion would be as costly as D-Day itself. Antwerp is desperately important, but it cannot be bought at such a high cost in lives."

"Is an air-borne assault out of the question?" asked the Air Commodore.

"Not altogether, but if it were not immediately and dramatically successful, we would find it nearly impossible to keep our troops on the ground supplied. The German's have deliberately flooded large areas, putting many roads under water. You must understand that Walcheron is like a huge soup bowl, ten miles in diameter. The whole central area is below sea-level. Over the centuries, the Dutch have reclaimed it, but only ceaseless pumping and careful maintenance of the dikes and sea-defences keep it habitable. Whilst I am sure we could send in paratroops, there is a significant risk they could be militarily successful initially, only to be starved into surrender. I think we have to go in from the sea, which I admit is not going to be easy. The alternative would be an attack from the land-ward side. This would be nearly as difficult as one from the sea. The ideal would be to land troops in the west. If the Canadians can push the Germans who are holding the south bank far enough eastward, they could simultaneously cross the Scheldt from the south, all at the same time as our army coming north from Belgium attack by land from the east."

"Have we an accurate assessment of the strength of the forces we're up against?" one of the captains asked.

"You touch on a sore point there, I'm afraid. It seems our intelligence sources in Holland have been infiltrated by the Germans and we've been led a merry dance by them in recent months. The whole resistance net-work has been compromised to the point where we don't know who to trust. There is no chance of re-establishing a dependable intelligence network. The only thing we can do is to send in our own independent agents to work in total isolation from any Dutch groups.

That is the only way we can be sure of getting accurate up-to-date intelligence. However, with no ground support from the Dutch Resistance, we can't parachute anyone in. They'd be picked up in no time, put up against a wall and shot.

"Sooner or later, we'll have to invade, but before we do, we do need to know the location and size of the mine-fields and the extent of the under-water obstructions on the beaches west of the port of Flushing. The idea we're working on now is that the RAF," here he nodded to the Air Commodore, "will pound the sea defences on the west side of Walcheron. If they can hack a big enough gap in the dikes, we can flood the hinterland. Whatever else that does, it will severely restrict the Nazis' ability to reinforce and re-supply their gun-emplacements. With any luck, we can then also send in troop-landing craft right through the gaps to attack them from the land-ward side. The assumption is that the Germans will have very little defence capability on the landward side because, quite naturally, they expect any attack to come from the sea. Possibly we can also use tank-landing craft to get amphibious tanks into action. However, you can see why it's so important that we're informed about mines and other defences."

"How will you know how successful our bombers have been in creating a gap in the dike?"

someone asked. "The RAF will be able to get aerial photos but, whilst they will show the breadth of any breaches, they won't help much when what we need to know is the depth of water."

"We'll immediately send in some of our special troops on motor torpedo boats. They should be able to get fairly close to the shore without being detected. Raiding parties can then go ashore in inflatables and collect information. What they can't do is to map the mine-fields. We do know the river is mined, but, equally, we know that the Germans are sending supplies across to their besieged comrades on the south side. They're using motorised barges, so there must be at least some considerable corridors through the mine-field. The Canadians and the Polish Armoured Division are slowly working their way along the south side of the Scheldt. At present we reckon it will be at least three weeks before we can get to a point where we might be able to embark a force of commandos to cross the river to Walcheron and take the port of Flushing on the north side. However, everything depends on knowing the extent of the mine-field."

"And how do we find that out?"

"Gentlemen! Let me introduce Lieutenant Huw Morgan of the Special Boat Squadron. Lieutenant, I've invited you here because I think you've an important contribution to make to this whole exercise. First, for the benefit of my colleagues here, I'll give a brief resume of your career to date. You volunteered at the out-break of hostilities. You were trained in diving and have considerable experience of under-water work. You reconnoitred the French beaches prior to D-Day. You have been doing concentrated training with the new motor submersible canoes. I see from your file, that you have a good grasp of both Flemish and Dutch. Have you any other languages?"

"I'm very fluent in Welsh, having been brought up in the Rhondda Valley. I am quite good at German, although I could never be mistaken for a German. I also have a smattering of French."

"The Dutch and the Flemish may be helpful. From your experience, how feasible does this sound? You are to be taken by submarine to a point three miles off the coast at the mouth of the Scheldt. There, you take a motor submersible canoe up the river and establish a base for yourself somewhere in the mud-flats. From your base, you explore the mine-fields and radio back their positions. A normal MSC would have insufficient range. A special craft is being built and will be ready before the end of the week. It's fully half as long again as an MSC Mark 2 you are familiar with. It also has a wider beam. Consequently it will have more than three times the battery power. This means that you should have an adequate power source both for the wireless and the boat. You'll not be carrying explosives so there will be plenty of room for food supplies for three weeks. You'll have to have completed your work within that time so that should be ample. Any questions?"

"One immediate problem is that, whilst I've some knowledge of the Morse Code, I'm no wireless expert."

"I know that. We'll arrange a special course for you and train you in codes. There's little time, but I'm sure you'll manage. Anything else?"

"When my work's done, how do I get out?"

"Ah! That's a problem. We cannot hope to take you out the way you went in. The chances of a submarine managing to rendezvous successfully with such a small boat make that out of the question. Apart from that, the mouth of the River Scheldt is likely to be a very busy and a very dangerous place by the time your work is done. We thought you might land on the south bank of the Scheldt, scuttle the MSC and make your way south through Holland into Belgium until you can make contact with the Canadians."

He makes it sound so simple, thought Huw. Despite massive misgivings, however, he heard himself accepting the assignment.

Chapter 4

The next few days were filled with frantic activity. Huw was taken that very afternoon in a Royal Navy Humber to a top-secret location in Hampshire. There, the whole of a country manor-house and its grounds had been requisitioned and now housed a major wireless unit. Tall aerials towered above the venerable walls. All the buildings bristled with antenna of various shapes and sizes. Huw was quartered in a nissen hut behind the old stable-block. Each day began with several hours of Morse Code practice. Already familiar with Morse, very soon Huw achieved a reasonably fast speed. He knew that the messages he sent here were being transmitted, not by wireless, but by land-lines to someone somewhere else in the complex. It was explained to him that his opposite number would always be the same person, someone highly skilled in reading and sending Morse. It was also explained that the two would never meet and would be known to each other only by their four letter code names. Personal contact was not only discouraged; it was forbidden. The explanation was that it was best to keep the relationship as impersonal as possible and to keep to a strict 'need to know' regime. Huw's code name was PGRB. His contact was SMFK. Who SMFK was, he had no idea. A man? A woman? Older? Younger? More senior rank? Lower rank? He hadn't a clue.

One thing he did know was the person at the other end was an expert, capable of transmitting far faster than he could receive; capable, too, of identifying Huw's 'fist', the peculiar and totally individual way he transmitted. This skill in confirming the identity of the person transmitting was invaluable. Whilst all messages carried certain code words whose inclusion or omission could warn the receiver that the agent had been captured and was transmitting under duress, the positive identification of the peculiar 'fist' of an agent ensured that no enemy could ever successfully take over his identity. The lessons painfully learnt in recent months in the Netherlands where the Dutch Resistance had been so effectively infiltrated by the Germans were evidently being strictly put into practice.

When he was not practising Morse, Huw was being instructed in the use of codes. It was vital to his survival that he transmit for the shortest time possible in order to give German wireless direction finders no chance of locating his position. Much of the code was based on the ancient Naval signalling system that went back not merely to pre-wireless days, but were in use before the Battle of Trafalgar. In those far-off days, ships at sea communicated by flying flags. Whilst obviously any message could be spelt out letter by letter with the twenty-six distinctive flags that represented the alphabet, the International Code of Signals enabled quite complex messages to be transmitted by the use of only two or three flags. The great advantage for Huw was that he could, for instance, send a message which identified him by his code, PGRB, then spelt out a single letter and a single number that identified a geographical area on a grid-map of the Scheldt estuary followed by a single letter meaning either 'Yes' or 'No' to indicate the presence of mines - C for 'Yes', N for 'No'. As the total transmitting time would be less than a minute, there was no real risk of being overheard, let alone of having his position pin-pointed.

There was perhaps less need for messages sent from England to him to be condensed as his position could not be located whilst he was receiving, as opposed to transmitting. Nevertheless, a similar series of codes were to be used. If nothing else, it would conserve battery power.

This crash course in signalling lasted less than a week. Then Huw was introduced to 'Sleeping Beauty'. 'Sleeping Beauty' was the latest in motor submersible canoes. At twenty-two feet in length, she was much larger than the MSCs Huw had previously trained on. In a restricted area west of Portsmouth, he put her through her paces. She handled perfectly and he soon found he could creep along with just his head above the surface with scarcely a ripple. The longer hull meant that 'Sleeping Beauty' had much larger banks of batteries than a standard MSC and these were reckoned to be able to provide both motive power and sufficient electricity for the wireless set for the three weeks his mission was expected to take. Water-tight containers, stored in lockers within the hull, could adequately carry the food and camping equipment necessary to sustain him for those three weeks. And, of course, there were water-tight containers for the wireless equipment.

During the third week of September, Huw was given a final briefing by Rear-Admiral Timpson.

"The Germans on the south bank are making the Canadians pay dearly for every yard they gain. However, our friends from Canada should be in a position to mount an attack across the Scheldt to

Flushing by early next month. This is, of course, only practical if we know where the mine-fields are in the river and how well fortified the northern bank is. The RAF are going to bomb the western sea-dikes of Walcheron within the next ten days. We will warn you the day before by repeatedly broadcasting your call-sign followed by the letter 'U' - the time-honoured signal for 'You are heading into danger.' When you get that, make sure you are well clear of the island. The bombing may not be all that accurate. Besides which, if a near-miss hits one of the mine-fields, there could be a pretty big under-water explosion. It would be better if you were able to take cover ashore somewhere, just to be sure."

"When do I leave, sir?" asked Huw.

"Tomorrow morning. Your MSC is being transported to Dover today in a special crate. This will be craned directly on to the rear casing of a submarine and anchored there. The length of the boat makes it impossible for the submarine to take the MSC below deck, beside which, the extra batteries she carries would mean quite heavy lifting gear being needed to launch her. The submarine will have to cross the Channel submerged and at half-speed to ensure no harm comes to the deck cargo. You should be off the Scheldt at night-fall. The submarine will nose its way up the channel but, because of the potential hazard of mine-fields, she will have to leave you several miles off Walcheron. If the sub comes up so that only her conning tower breaks the surface, German radar is most unlikely to detect her. A couple of divers will help you dismantle the crate under water and you should be then able to float clear of the sub.

"The priority after that will be to press on up river under cover of darkness. The fore-cast is for a force two westerly and high-tide is 0540 hours. The wind and the flowing tide will help you. There will be a moderate swell, but nothing to worry an MSC. With the wind behind you and going with the tide, you should be off Flushing by 0300 hours. You will need to find somewhere to hole up before day-light. The south bank is broken up with mud-flats and sand-banks. There are deep creeks between them and drainage ditches which, in some cases, penetrate a couple of miles or more inland. I needn't remind you that you will need to be very careful. I expect you can get your MSC well under the cover of the mud-banks. However, you might find yourself up a creek and unable to turn. Coming out astern will be tricky, to say the least. "

Huw thought for a moment. "No doubt we have all the Admiralty charts, but they won't show any detail of the mud-flats. Have we any decent maps of them?"

"Nothing which will help you much, I'm afraid. The Dutch equivalent of our Ordnance Survey maps show very little detail. We have some more drawings published in the twenties by one of the international ornithological societies, but they are very sketchy. Besides which, none of us knows if the sand-banks and mud-flats have changed significantly in the last twenty years. I'm sorry, but you're very much on your own this time."

"So it seems! I'll give it my best shot, but I can't promise you anything. I'd better pick up the maps and charts and spend this afternoon memorising them. It's hardly worth taking them all with me. It's not as though I can navigate with the map spread out in front of me!"

"Well, thanks, Morgan. You're a brave man and, if anyone can see this one through, I'm sure you can. We'll notify the Canadians so that they'll be expecting you. I'll give you personal pass-words so that you can get them to radio us to confirm your identity."

With that, the two men parted. Huw spent the rest of the day pouring over maps. Later that afternoon, the big Humber, driven by a Wren, carried him comfortably through the south of England to Dover harbour.

Chapter 5

Dover harbour was shrouded in mist as the submarine nosed its way out into the English Channel just after dawn. A light rain was falling and visibility was reduced to a couple of hundred yards. Huw stood in the conning tower with the submarine's commander. He looked out astern, past the strange, long, slim, torpedo-shaped crate on the rear casing. The famous white cliffs were visible for only a few seconds, then the vessel was surrounded only by the eerie whiteness of the mist. Several minutes later, the conning tower was cleared and the submarine slipped quietly below the surface. Huw shared breakfast with the senior officers but conversation was somewhat stilted. The 'need to know' principle meant that there could be no discussion about his mission. Furthermore, so much of his war up to that point had been cloaked in secrecy, that he was unable to share experiences with his temporary companions. By mid-morning, he was quite glad of the excuse that he should try to get some sleep, in view of what lay ahead that night. He did not sleep, however. The stuffy atmosphere and the continual noise and movement of men in the confined space of the submarine made him toss and turn sleeplessly on the narrow bunk allocated to him.

Late in the afternoon, he ate a hearty meal, reflecting gloomily on the fact that, if all went to plan, this would be the last hot meal he would have for three weeks. If all did not go to plan, it would be the last hot meal he would ever have.

At 2200 hours, the submarine's motors stopped and the gentle heaving of the hull told Huw that they had surfaced. After struggling into his diving suit, he climbed up the conning-tower ladder and looked around. The sky had cleared and the slender crescent of a new moon cast a sickly light on an empty sea. A light breeze blew in from the west, rippling the surface of the long, low waves that washed over the still submerged casing fore and aft of the conning-tower.

"Walcheron's about five miles over there," said the commander. "With our head height being only about fifteen feet above the sea, we should be completely hidden by the curvature of the earth in broad day-light so there's no risk of us being spotted, especially at night. An alert radar operator might just notice a tiny stationary blip, but we'll be here for only a few minutes. By the time he refers it to someone higher, the blip will have gone."

They looked over the conning-tower. The two divers had already nearly completed dismantling the crate.

"About time I went," said Huw. Both of them were speaking in whispers, such was the tension in the conning tower. Huw smiled to himself at this ridiculous precaution.

"Well, the very best of luck! We'll slip below the surface as soon as you've floated clear but we'll be watching you by periscope. Only once we're sure you're well on your way will we start the motors so there'll be no risk of us capsizing you."

The two men shook hands. Huw pulled on his helmet and scrambled down the ladder to the rear casing. 'Sleeping Beauty' was just under the surface, the long, low swell sweeping over her. One of the divers gave him a 'thumbs up' and he settled himself in the cockpit. The diver released the last mountings that secured the MSC to the submarine and the next wave carried the small craft clear. In the cockpit, the light on the instrument panel glowed comfortingly. Checking his compass-bearing, Huw swung the boat forward. As he settled on his course, he turned to give a last wave to the submarine but she had already slipped below the surface, leaving only an empty sea. A great sense of loneliness and foreboding swept over him.

It was so dark that Huw felt completely safe running on the surface. With what wind there was coming from behind him, he made good time and after three hours or so, he sensed, rather than saw, land on both sides. If he were right, he must be in the relatively narrow part of the estuary, with the port of Flushing somewhere on his left, perhaps a mile or two away. He cut the motor and eased off his helmet. The estuary was almost a flat calm. Listening carefully, he could detect the slight hum of machinery and vehicles, for all the world like a distant bee-hive. He could see nothing of the port, so the Germans must have enforced a very strict blackout. As he had to be sure of his position, Huw steered northwards with the motor running at its lowest speed. Gradually he could hear more. The sound of engines and the occasional human voice echoed over the oily calm water.

Satisfied he knew where he was, Huw turned the MSC and headed slowly and silently southwards. Suddenly he became aware of the throb of a heavy engine. Peering through the gloom, he saw first, the phosphorescence of a bow wave, then the blunt bows of a large motorised barge charging towards him. He pulled on his helmet, adjusted the air supply and took 'Sleeping Beauty' down. At thirty feet, he levelled the craft out and shut the motor down. Above him, he could hear the pulsating sound of the barge's propeller. Confident he had not been spotted, he waited for it to pass. The engine note above him increased in volume steadily, then, at last, began to fade. He realised he had learnt something important already. The barge was no doubt supplying the besieged German forces in the pocket they still held on the south side of the Scheldt. There was obviously a mine-free corridor between Flushing on the north and Breskens on the south bank.

Huw steered 'Sleeping Beauty' eastwards, reckoning that he was more or less in the middle of the navigational channel. Still running at thirty feet down, he pressed on at a steady two knots in nearly total darkness. Suddenly, the MSC juddered and swung to port. Clearly, she had stuck something. Huw put the motor astern and, with a slight tremor, she came free. Very gently, he eased her ahead and starboard a little. As the craft moved ahead, he could feel her scraping past something. As it came level with the cockpit, he realised it was the mooring cable of a mine. He had passed from the safe corridor into a mine-field.

At his last briefing, Huw had been told that the mine-fields were his friends. There was so little ferrous metal in the construction of an MSC that there was no chance of detonating a magnetic mine. Similarly, unless he had the misfortune to run smack into an unstable contact mine, the light boat would not set one off. Meanwhile, in a mine-field, he would be safe from German surface craft. It had sounded good in the naval lecture theatre back at Portsmouth. Here, looking up the cable, he could just discern the ominous dark shape above and the argument seemed strangely less convincing.

Once the MSC was clear of the cable, Huw pressed the twin switches that let compressed air into the buoyancy tanks fore and aft. Just a gentle squirt and 'Sleeping Beauty' began to rise very slowly. As he neared the surface, Huw was able to see more. On the way up he passed two mines. The one whose cable he had struck was only feet away whilst the other was a dim shape a few yards ahead. With scarcely a ripple the small boat broke the surface. Ahead, to the east, the sky was already quite light. However, he seemed to be shrouded in darkness to left, right and astern. He glanced at his watch. Five ten. The tide would be turning and full daylight must be only an hour away. It was high time to find a refuge for the coming daylight hours.

Swinging 'Sleeping Beauty' shore-wards, he adjusted the hydroplanes and the hull slipped below the surface, leaving only his head above water. At slow speed, Huw took the craft in towards the reed-covered mud-banks on the south side of the river. Following a creek between two small islets, he found himself in a small lagoon, surrounded by high reeds. Gently, he beached the MSC and eased himself out of the cockpit and on to a shingle-covered strand about six feet wide that extended round the islet, forming a border between the water and the reeds. Pulling off his helmet, he crawled into the reeds. Very cautiously, he raised himself until, in kneeling position, he could just see over the reeds. His island was perhaps fifty yards long and twenty across. Nowhere was it more than two feet above the high-water mark. Northward, he could just see the smudge that was the shore-line of Walcheron on the other side of the Scheldt. Southwards, what appeared to be the shore was fully a quarter of a mile away across a mixture of water and ooze, interspersed with reed covered banks like his own.

This would do as temporary shelter. It would have to do. The sky was lightening by the minute and the signs were that a sunny day lay ahead. He would have to hole up here until an hour or so before high-tide in the afternoon. Then, certain he had plenty of depth of water, he could begin his work of mapping the mine-field. Whilst this would do as a base for one night, he did not want to settle on it as a more permanent one, if only because, with no distinctive land-marks, he might not find his way back to it. The trouble was that the whole coastline was rather featureless.

Huw opened 'Sleeping Beauty's' lockers and recovered water-tight containers holding food, water, a ground sheet, a sleeping-bag and camouflage netting. He then pushed the craft off the beach and took her into the centre of the lagoon. There, he submerged her, riding down with her until she bottomed in soft mud at fifteen feet. That meant there was a slight chance she might break surface at low tide but there was nothing he could do about that. She could not be seen from the shore and he had been assured that there was virtually no German activity in the air as the Allies enjoyed total air supremacy over Belgium and much of Holland. He swam to the shore and soon established a carefully concealed hiding place in the reeds. Gratefully wriggling out of the diving-suit, Huw lay in the rays of the rising sun until the perspiration had dried off his clothing. Then he crawled into his sleeping bag and, surprisingly, was soon asleep.

Chapter 6

The sun was high in the sky when Huw awoke. For several minutes he lay, basking in its warmth and listening to the sound of the salt marshes - the song of birds, the ripple of wavelets and the swish of the lightest of breezes in the reeds. Suddenly the war seemed a thousand miles away. Dragging himself back to reality, he slipped out of his sleeping bag and, with infinite care, parted the reeds so that he could see northwards across the river. The tide was nearly flat out, exposing the mud-flats and sand-banks ahead as well as to left and right. Apart from flocks of birds, some in the water, some airborne, nothing stirred. Farther up river, about a mile away, he could see a rusting hulk rising out of the mud. Although it must be nearly covered at high tide, he thought it might provide the conspicuous land-mark he would need to guide him to whatever he was going to use as a base for the next three weeks or so. As soon as there was enough water, he would recover 'Sleeping Beauty' and investigate. Meanwhile, he wriggled round and surveyed the nearer shoreline to the south, a monotonous series of mud-banks with the higher points crowned with reeds. The presence of so many sea-birds was reassuring. As they wheeled, dived and landed on the shore, it was clear there were no human beings moving in the vicinity.

As soon as the tide had risen sufficiently, Huw donned his diving suit and slipped into the water. He quickly located the MSC and brought her to the surface. A few minutes later, having loaded his scanty equipment on her, he cautiously steered out of the lagoon. He followed the line of the creek by which he had entered and was soon running with only his head above water towards the wreck up-river. As he neared it, he shut the motor down and let the momentum carry his craft gently alongside. The vessel had been some kind of river barge, about ninety feet long and thirty wide. It had obviously suffered catastrophic damage and had been hurriedly beached. The old steel hull was rent in several places and an explosion had blown the whole bow section several feet higher than it should have been. Only the top six feet of the bows would be above water at high tide, as the line of weed and other marine growth on the rest of the hull made clear. The hulk lay nearly parallel to the shore-line, separated from it by quarter of a mile of juicy mud at low tide. The barge was listing out into the river and the mud had built up on the shore-ward side, whilst the other side was obviously scoured clear by each tide. Huw flooded the buoyancy tanks and nosed the MSC under the overhanging hull. The rising tide carried his craft gently upstream alongside the heavily fouled plates of the wreck. As he approached the bows, Huw saw the massive hole blasted in the ship's side that had so nearly blown the bow section away. Catching at the jagged metal, he slowed the progress of the MSC and secured her to a damaged rib with a stout mooring line. A second line lashing the two dissimilar craft together added to his peace of mind as he slid out of the cockpit and, guided by a small, waterproof torch, entered the hull.

Everything was covered in silt, but, looking upwards, he could see daylight filtering down through

the murky water. Very carefully, he worked his way upwards, eventually surfacing through a jagged tear in the steel into what had once been the chain-locker. The light he had seen from below entered through the ports for the anchor chain and also through a long slit in the decking above. The heavy links of chain were now welded together with rust and formed a very uneven floor in the claustrophobic space. It was far from ideal, but it certainly had possibilities. From the starboard anchor-chain port, he could get a very limited view of the shore. The corresponding port on the sea-ward side was practically useless as all he could see was the surface of the water below. Huw decided he would try spending that night in the hulk. Meanwhile, he wanted to use the remaining daylight hours to survey the mine-field.

Once back in 'Sleeping Beauty', Huw headed northwards, gradually taking the craft deeper, following the bed of the river. Quite abruptly, the bottom shelved away steeply and he found himself at thirty feet with no bottom in sight. Equally suddenly, he found himself in the mine field. The sunlight filtered down and through the gloom, he could just make out anchor cables here and there and, above them, the sinister cylindrical and spherical shapes of the mines themselves. He assumed the entire breadth of the navigable channel would be fairly uniformly mined, so he turned downstream and gently weaved his way past the cables until suddenly he was clear of them. This meant that he was now in the mine-free corridor. To identify where its eastern limit was, he would have to surface and try to get some sort of bearing. Then it would be a matter of going downstream submerged until he found the western limit. The moment of greatest risk would be as he broke surface. The only consolation was that there would be no German craft in the mine-field area. He squirted air into the tanks until the MSC just started to rise. The daylight gradually increased. He could see the surface above, so he released a little air to slow his ascent and his head broke the surface. Hurriedly, he looked round. Not a boat to be seen and both shores a couple of miles away.

To the northwest, he could make out the jib of a crane and a factory chimney. That must be Flushing! To the southwest, barely visible and farther away was a church-spire. He assumed that would be Breskens. Very carefully, he took a compass-bearing on each, noting them down on the water-proof pad that was slung round his neck. Up-river on the north bank was a ruinous wind-mill. He took a bearing on it for good measure. As quietly as he had surfaced, he slipped below the waves again. The tide was on the turn and he made steady progress down river. An hour and a half elapsed and he was suddenly confronted with mines again. Gently, he surfaced. This time he could see a motor boat a mile or more away. As only his head was above water, he felt reasonably secure. Even if an alert pair of eyes did spot something it would be a brave skipper who came charging into a known mine-field to investigate. Once again, he took bearings on the same land-marks in Flushing and Breskens.

Satisfied with his progress, he set a course for Flushing and took 'Sleeping Beauty' down to twenty feet. Estimating his speed at three miles an hour and the port nearly three miles away, he let 45 minutes elapse before very gently approaching the surface. This time he levelled off with his head about two feet below the surface. He shut down the motor and strained his ears for any sound of engines or propellers. Nothing! Only an eerie silence. Involuntarily holding his breath, he broke the surface. The tide had carried him downstream more than he had expected, but Flushing was now clearly visible, a mile or so upstream. Above him on the shore were the heavy guns of two substantial shore-batteries, no doubt manned by very alert sentries.

Quickly getting a fix on a sewer pipe running over the sand and into the river, he submerged and nosed his way gently towards it. The bottom was shoaling fast, so Huw adjusted his course to run parallel to the shore.

He reckoned the outlet of the sewer would be under water at low tide so, if he could secure 'Sleeping Beauty' to it, he would be sure she would not be left high and dry as the tide ebbed. He could also be sure that he would be able to find her again without difficulty. Although he was now running with his head a bare two feet below the surface, visibility became steadily poorer. To his disgust, Huw realised he was now navigating through a stream of raw sewage. Fighting down the inevitable nausea, he followed the line of the increasingly dense muck until he arrived at the end of the sewer pipe. He swung the bows of the MSC out into the river and cautiously moved the boat astern until she was lying alongside the pipe some six feet from the outlet. There, he moored her to the pipe and eased himself out of the cockpit.

The pipe was covered with a prolific growth of sea-weed that waved gently in the swell. Taking advantage of the cover it provided, Huw carefully raised his head above the surface. The shore was only fifty yards away and, a quarter of a mile from him and walking towards the pipe, were two German soldiers, each with a rifle slung on his shoulder. Huw shrank back and watched the two approach. The men were obviously relaxed and deep in conversation. When they reached the pipe, they stopped and lit cigarettes. Then they continued along the beach, eventually disappearing up a gap in the dunes. Very kind of them, thought Huw. They had conveniently confirmed that this stretch of beach was not mined. All he had to do now was to check for 'hedgehogs' or other under-water obstructions designed to prevent a sea-borne assault.

Huw returned to 'Sleeping Beauty' and soon was slowly patrolling along parallel to the shore at a distance that he guessed corresponded with the low tide line. After half a mile heading downstream, he reversed his course and, now a farther hundred yards out in the river, he moved back upstream. No obstructions at all! Apart from the awe-inspiring presence of the battery of heavy guns, this would be the place for a landing.

Taking a course that would have him pass Flushing a quarter of a mile out in the river, Huw took 'Sleeping Beauty' down and followed the bed of the river. As he expected, the harbour mouth was free of mines, but, farther up the river, he found himself again negotiating his way through a thin forest of mooring cables. The tide was ebbing now and he could feel the MSC struggling to make way against it. After an hour, he surfaced. He was now comfortably upstream from Flushing and half a mile out into the river. Quickly establishing his bearings, he submerged again and headed for the islets in the mud-flats on the south side. He knew he would need to watch his time. The evening was setting in and he was anxious to radio England whilst still leaving himself adequate time to get to the wreck before night-fall.

Huw reached the shallows and eased the craft upwards. His head broke the surface and a quick look round reassured him. The sea-birds were circling round or fishing here and there. The atmosphere of total tranquillity convinced him that there was no-one around. He slid into a lagoon and found a place to land. It took several minutes to compose his message, giving a detailed report on his discoveries to date. Moving as quickly as he could, he rigged his aerial and soon was tapping out his call-sign - PGRB, PGRB, PGRB - over and over again for half a minute. Then came the reply - SMFK, SMFK, SMFK. Quickly, but carefully, Huw tapped out his message. As soon as he got 'Received and understood', he signed off and packed the wireless back in its watertight compartment. The chances of being overheard were quite high and the strength of the signal would alert the Nazis to the presence of someone sending messages from somewhere close to, or actually in, Flushing. However, there was no risk of them having got a 'fix' on his position on this first occasion. That danger would increase with each time he broadcast and the future would become steadily more perilous. In fading light, he reached the barge and secured 'Sleeping

Beauty' under the overhang of the hull. The chain locker was almost totally in darkness but he did not dare use his torch. Instead, he groped his way around, inflated his rubber mattress and, having pulled off his diving suit, he gratefully settled down in his sleeping bag.

Chapter 7

Dawn came late the next day, heavy cloud and rain squalls obscuring any view across the river. Huw peered out of the anchor-port, but could barely discern the coastline. The miserable day, with its poor visibility, would be of immense help to him. He decided that this would be a good opportunity to reconnoitre the defences of the western side of Walcheron down at the mouth of the Scheldt. With such limited visibility, he could ride the ebb tide on the surface with minimal risk of being detected and with the probability of reaching his destination in a couple of hours. This would be less than half the time it would take submerged and, perhaps more importantly, it would enable him to conserve battery power. After a hurried breakfast, he donned his diving suit and worked his way aft to where 'Sleeping Beauty' lay on the bottom. He took her out into mid-stream before surfacing. The rain was still falling gently as he slipped his helmet off. Switching off the motor, he kept absolutely still, listening. Beyond the soft ripple of the river and the occasional cry of a sea-bird, he could hear the distant rumble of vehicles in and around Flushing, but nothing else.

Huw paddled the MSC down the river at a steady, silent rate. The noise of the port, shrouded in the murk a mile off to starboard, grew louder. Then, as it slipped astern, the noises of the river began to dominate. The ebb tide was now carrying him steadily sea-wards. Correcting his course, he followed the shore-line just far enough out for him to be sure that not even an alert sentry would see him. Once he was sure he had come far enough down-stream, he shipped his paddle, pulled on his helmet and quietly took his craft down to the point where only his head was above water. Running at half speed, he approached the shore. The grey smudge of land grew steadily clearer. Directly ahead, he could see

the massive earth-works of one of the many shore-batteries, the barrels of its heavy guns trained on the distant horizon. It was an awe-inspiring sight. If these guns were not rapidly put out of action, any invading force would be torn to pieces before a single soldier set foot on land. Adjusting his course, Huw brought 'Sleeping Beauty' ashore half a mile from the battery. As she grounded, he slipped out of the cockpit and secured the MSC to the sand with a grapnel. The tide was on the turn now, so he was confident the boat would stay undetected.

The beach was utterly deserted. There were no underwater defences between the low and high-water marks but there was no easy way of knowing if the beach between the high water mark and the steeply-rising dike beyond was mined. Trailing a marker line behind him, Huw swam ashore. Lying in the surf, he waited for a rain-squall to sweep along the beach and then crawled up to the high watermark. From there on, he would have to probe for mines and try to assess whether landing-craft could safely disgorge their men here. He had only moved forward a few feet when there was burst of rifle fire and the sand beside him was flung in the air as a salvo of bullets spattered around him. He flung himself sideways as another fusillade struck the beach where he had lain only a second before. He glanced up and saw a group of five soldiers at the top of the dike only a couple of hundred yards away. Worse still, racing down the steep side of the dike were two massive dogs. Huw turned and ran. He heard the growl of the dogs and wondered, as he ran, whether he had any chance of out-running them or whether he should face them with his knife. If the dogs did not get him, the rifles surely would. The nearest dog must be almost on his heels. He drew his knife, wheeled and crouched. The dog, now less than thirty yards away, was rocketing towards him when suddenly there was an almighty explosion that swept him off his feet. The mine blew the dog to pieces and Huw struggled to his feet as sand and bloody fragments of dog spattered around and upon him. The second dog wheeled round and, tail between its legs, ran back up the dike.

Before the dust had settled, Huw had recovered from the shock and was on his feet, running for his life over the wet sand and into the surf. The startled Germans also recovered and bullets whistled past him and splashed into the water beside him. Miraculously, he was not hit. He stumbled into deeper water, took a deep breath and did a shallow dive. The bottom was only three feet down. Huw swung round to swim parallel to the shore, groping as he did so for the line that would guide him back to 'Sleeping Beauty'. He found it, lay on his back and, pushing his hands on the firm sand below, forced his face above the surface long enough to get a lung-full of fresh air. Then he pulled himself under and onwards with the line until he reached the MSC. Confident the enemy would not venture down to the water-line through the mine-field, he grabbed his helmet and stood up. He had almost succeeded in pulling it on when a shout and the crackle of rifle fire told him he had been spotted. He ducked down and adjusted the air-flow under the water, not the normal procedure but by far the best in these circumstances.

Turning 'Sleeping Beauty' seawards, Huw tried to guess what the Germans would do. Provided they thought he had come from the sea, perhaps from a British submarine lying a few miles off-shore, they would send surface craft to hunt for him. If they had a suitable submarine hunter, they would try to depth-charge the hypothetical submarine. As soon as he was in deep enough water, Huw turned up-stream. After a mile for so, he heard the roar of approaching engines and the churning of fast-rotating propellers. He turned shore-wards into shallow water. In only five feet, he settled the MSC on the bottom and waited for the noise to reach a crescendo and then recede. Then he nosed out to deep water again. Another mile and he reached the comparative safety of the mine-field. It was strangely comforting to be surrounded by the mooring cables and to see the dim shapes of the mines eerily floating above him.

Slowly he made his way upstream, porpoising every fifteen minutes to correct his course. Once he was well clear of Flushing, he steered out into the middle of the channel and allowed the flood-tide to sweep him upstream. A couple of miles past the hulk, with squalls of rain spattering constantly around him, he nosed his way towards the narrow channel between Walcheron and South Beveland. This was one of his potential escape routes, depending on whether the Allies made better progress along the north bank of the Scheldt than they did along the south. The channel, he knew, practically dried out at low tide, leaving an almost impassable ditch whose bottom was a virtual quicksand of juicy mud. Barbed wire entanglements were strung across the mouth of the channel, but, although they were fairly dense, he reckoned he could, if he had to, cut his way through underwater at high tide. Beyond the barbed-wire barrier, there seemed to be very little by way of obstruction. As he drew near land, he pushed the joy-stick forwards and 'Sleeping Beauty' slipped under water. Then, suddenly, he was in a very dense mine-field. The Germans had obviously felt that there was little need for strong land-based defences when the shore was so thoroughly defended against a sea-borne invasion. Huw went deeper and brought the MSC round in a half-circle, weaving his way past a veritable forest of cables.

Two more miles up the river and Huw brought the craft ashore. The tide was well in and the north bank of the Scheldt, like the south lower down, was a broken series of mud-flats and marshy islands. Leaving 'Sleeping Beauty' submerged in six feet of water, he eased himself ashore and hid in the dense reeds on one of these islands. In a wide lagoon between him and the shore, a large flock of swans swam peacefully, occasionally sticking their heads underwater and their tails ridiculously in the air as they sought food on the muddy bottom. Farther off, a solitary heron stood on one leg, solemnly meditating on the world around him.

Convinced he was utterly alone, Huw slipped back into the water and brought his wireless set ashore. He tuned in and picked up a steady stream of Morse. PGRB U PGRB U PGRB U. The same message over and over again for five minutes, then a two minute break before the same message was repeated. U! The international 'you are running into danger' signal, but for Huw it carried a special meaning. The air-raids on Walcheron's dikes would begin tomorrow!

Carefully, Huw composed his own messages

about mined and unmined beaches. He waited for the next two minute break in SMFK's transmission. Then he started calling PGRB to SMFK. PGRB to SMFK Once he received confirmation, he broadcast his message as quickly as the need for absolute accuracy would permit. He breathed a sigh of relief as he got 'Received and understood.' He signed off and dismantled the equipment. Suddenly there was a strange rushing sound. He looked sideways up and saw the skein of swans taking off over his head, flying only eight feet or so above him. He looked shore-wards and saw fifty or sixty soldiers, complete with dogs, deploying along the distant shore and starting to sweep outwards through the shallow water.

Huw shrank back and, dragging his wireless in its water-proof container behind him, he slipped into the water. In minutes, he had 'Sleeping Beauty' submerged and moving noiselessly across the river. The roar of high-speed engines warned him of the approach of motor-launches, but, twenty feet below the surface, he felt reasonably secure. He checked his compass and steered west down the river. After a couple of miles, he cautiously took the MSC up. There was no sound of boats so he gently broke surface. The rain was torrential now and visibility was down to a hundred yards or so, a mixed blessing as he was unsure of his precise position.

With only his head above water, he turned south. At half speed, he approached the shore. Soon he found himself in a virtual archipelago of muddy islands. Visibility was no better and so he decide to land on a particularly densely-reeded island and await an improvement in the weather. There was no hope of finding the barge in this murk.

Chapter 8

The rain did moderate as the evening went on. Through the gloom of late evening, Huw could make out the dark silhouette of the barge quarter of a mile downstream He, himself, was on one of the farthest out of the reed-covered mud-banks on the south side, an uncomfortable place to spend the night. Just as he was deciding to move to the barge, two motor boats came into view on the north side of the Scheldt. Each was laden with heavily armed soldiers and the two boats were going from islet to islet, dropping off parties of men at the top of each and picking them up at the bottom after they had combed their way through the reeds. Along the shore beyond them, similar groups of men swarmed through the dunes and over the dikes, these being accompanied by dogs. It was all too clear that Huw must have broadcast his last message dangerously close to a direction-finding unit.

The concentrated search was, for the present, on the north side, but the chances were that, having failed there, the Germans would switch their attention to the islands along the south bank. Huw decided that the safest place to hole up for that night at least would be on one of the islets that had just been subjected to a thorough search on the north side. Accordingly, he slipped back into 'Sleeping Beauty' and re-crossed the river. Landing at a point a mile above the current German activity, he lay in the reeds and kept a discreet watch. Sure enough, at the western end of the chain of islets and sand-banks on the north side, the searchers crossed the river and began to work their way upstream. A substantial number of reinforcements joined them, presumably from Breskens, and started to comb the shore. The tide was now half out and there were perhaps two hours of daylight left.

One of the boats moored alongside the barge and several men boarded her. With difficulty, they made their way up the slime-covered, steeply-sloping deck to the bows. These were covered with guano and, as Huw had never climbed up on them, he was confident there would be no trace of his recent occupancy. One man was kneeling down, presumably peering through the crack in the decking. Knowing he had left no visible signs of his presence, Huw was not too worried. The soldiers held a brief consultation, then one leant over the side and tossed a grenade into the chain locker through the anchor-port. The muffled explosion rumbled across the river to where Huw lay. For good measure, they tossed several more into the hold and other submerged parts of the barge before retiring. Grateful he was not there, Huw continued to watch their progress up-river, moving from island to island, until, at last, they were lost in the failing light.

Huw slept fitfully. The island was very wet and it rained off and on during the night. He woke, aching in every limb and feeling stiff and sore. The eastern sky was just showing the first rays of morning sun when the skies started to throb with the sound of the unsilenced engines of heavy bombers. From the west they came, wave after wave of Halifaxes and Lancasters. To the roar of their mighty, unsilenced engines was soon added the heavy crump of high explosives as they poured their bomb-loads down on the dikes of Walcheron. To add to the bedlam of noise, the anti-aircraft batteries inland on the island opened up with much drama but little effect. The huge sea-defence batteries remained silent, absolutely impotent in the face of the attack from the skies. As the day wore on, the anti-aircraft guns one by one fell silent. Huw did not know at the time, but later learned that the sea, bursting through the shattered dikes, had made all roads impassable and flooded the gun-sites. Having dropped their loads, the massive bombers swung in an arc only a few hundred feet above Huw's head and set off on their return flight to England. A pang of envy swept through Huw as he thought of these men, who, a couple of hours later, would be sitting down to a slightly delayed hot breakfast. Meanwhile, he could hardly remember what a cooked meal was like.

The attack was relentlessly pressed home all day. To Huw, the aircraft seemed never-ending, streaming from the west, dropping their bombs and swinging southwards and westwards to home again. In the event, the RAF had deployed over 260 heavy bombers and had substantially destroyed the sea-defences of Walcheron, leaving the island ready for invasion.

Chapter 9

The invasion of Walcheron should have began during the first week of October, immediately after the destruction of the dikes. However, the German defence of the pocket they held on the south side of the River Scheldt was unexpectedly stubborn. It was so stubborn indeed, that it would not be until the third week of October that the Canadian 3rd Division, supported by the Polish Armoured Division, took Breskens. During the first ten days of October, Huw continued to survey the channel and the beaches, reporting at irregular intervals by wireless. Each time he contacted England, he was aware of the possibility of being pin-pointed by the Germans and he had the pessimistic feeling that his luck was running out.

Whether or not his luck was running out or not, his provisions certainly were. Whenever it rained, he was able to collect a little rain water so he could keep thirst at bay, but, despite strictly rationing his food supplies, he would soon have to go hungry. Then came the signal authorising his withdrawal. It had always been assumed that he would head south, perhaps even as far as Belgium, and then make contact with the advancing Allies. He had been told that the troops in this sector were mainly Canadian, although these were supported by Polish units. Huw hoped he would encounter the Canadians as there would clearly be a major communications problem if his first contact were to be with front-line Polish infantry.

Now that the time had come to move, it was obvious that the front line was very near. For several days the noise of heavy guns had continued day and night to the south and the east and the distant rumble of trucks and tanks could often be heard. The River Scheldt itself brought the evidence of fierce fighting up-stream as yet more corpses were washed down with every tide. The barge seemed to attract them, its torn metal hooking into the shreds of clothing as the remains of friend and foe alike were swept along on the ebb-tide.

It was therefore with no regret that Huw swam ashore an hour before dawn, pushing before him a water-tight container with dry clothes, his water bottle, his last tin of bully beef and the few remaining stale biscuits. Ashore, he dressed hurriedly and then headed inland. It was still dark. However, he had identified a deep drainage ditch that penetrated far inland. Following the line of this ditch which was one of many which drained the fen-like flat-lands to left and right, he hurried southwards. By day-break, he was three miles from the river and realised he was nearing the front-line. The problem of how to reach the Allied forces without being shot by either side was troubling him. At any moment, he might stumble into the rear of German forces. Then would come the difficulty of getting past them unnoticed. The admiral at the briefing meeting had not issued clear instructions on how this should be done, Huw thought wryly.

He struck out along a narrow ditch, keeping his head well down. At a point where the reeds almost bridged it above his head, he crawled up the bank and looked out over a flat meadow ahead. In the distance to the left were a row of tanks, advancing slowly, their engines giving a deep rumble. Allied or German? He lay still as they crawled from left to right about half a mile in front of him. As they came nearer, he could see the big white star painted on each. The Liberation Star! The standard marking on every Allied vehicle, be it American, Free French, British, Polish or whatever. Immense relief surged through him. Between and behind the tanks he could now make out infantry advancing at a crouching run.

Then, to his right, ahead of the advancing Allied force, a German waving a white flag climbed out of a ditch. The tanks stopped. Shouts, some recognisable to Huw as German, reached his ears. The other language he could not identify, so he assumed it to be Polish. There was a long shouted conversation, none of which Huw could make out clearly. Then more Germans, their hands high above their heads emerged from the ditch and slowly followed their flag-flying comrade, a dozen or more in total. Huw watched them walk forward and thought that, as soon as their surrender was complete, he would advance and make himself known.

The Germans reached a point perhaps twenty yards from the Polish line when a voice shouted in German, "Now!"

The Germans flung the grenades they had been holding, pins already removed, and threw themselves flat on the ground. Even before the grenades exploded, hidden machine-guns in the ditch behind them opened up, scything down the Polish soldiers. Then came the heavier crump of anti-tank guns and two of the Polish tanks erupted in flames. The remaining tanks burst into life, roaring forward with every gun blazing. The prostrate Germans rolled this way and that in an effort to avoid being ground to pulp under the tanks' tracks, but those who escaped being crushed soon found a Polish bullet or bayonet finishing them off.

Horrified, yet fascinated, Huw watched from his

ditch. The carnage was dreadful. A hundred or more men in total, German and Polish, must have died in the course of two minutes. As the noise started to tail off, Huw hurriedly retreated along the way he had come. He was desperately disappointed, but knew this was not a good day to try waving a white flag to Polish soldiers. Making the best speed he could whilst exercising considerable caution, Huw crawled for over an hour towards the river.

His caution proved amply justified. As he made his way along a drainage ditch, he suddenly heard the sound of running footsteps. He pressed himself down into the mud, drawing the long reeds over his body. Holding his breath he lay absolutely still. A soldier slid down into the ditch only a few yards from him. Then there were several more, mercifully farther along. Orders were passed along in harsh whispers. German! Huw was right on the German front line! Five minutes later the firing began. A machine-gun a mere ten yards from him opened up on what Huw had to presume were advancing Polish infantry. Then there was in-coming fire. Bullets whistled overhead. These were accompanied by mortar shells. Most of the shells struck one or other side of the ditch, with only the occasional one scoring a hit in the ditch itself. When this did happen, the result was very dramatic. Mud was thrown everywhere and shell-splinters whistled through the air.

However, the shells seemed to have driven themselves so far into the soft mud before exploding that they did little damage to the defending Germans.

Huw wondered how it would end. What he really dreaded was the possibility that the Poles would bring up flame-throwing tanks. There would be no chance of surviving no matter how well he was hidden. Meanwhile, all he could do was to try to sink as deeply into the mud as he could without actually drowning in it.

With the noise of battle all around him, Huw did not hear the sound of advancing troops until fifty or more Germans threw themselves into the ditch all around him. He would inevitably have been discovered at that point were it not for a burst of machine-gun fire which tore into the last of the soldiers as they sought cover in the ditch. A huge corporal, half his head blown away, collapsed into the ditch on top of Huw. His head forced right under the mud, Huw struggled to ease the weight off him without, at the same time, revealing his presence. He gasped for air, his mouth breaking the surface under the dead man's right shoulder. Blinded by the mud, yet unable to move his hand to clear it from his face without attracting attention, he could only wait. Minutes later, he heard the distant rumble of tanks. With only one ear out of the clinging mud, he could not locate the sound. Were the advancing tanks Polish or German?

Which would he prefer? Huw really did not know.

Above the roar of tank engines and the crackle of machine-gun fire came the sound of heavy guns. A dark shadow crossed Huw's very limited horizon. He realised that the tanks were German and were crossing the narrow ditch on both sides of him and practically above him. There was a shout and the surviving Germans rose to their feet and set off at a shambling trot behind the tanks. At least on this part of the front, the Polish advance was being driven remorselessly back. An eerie silence fell as the sounds of engines, shells and guns receded eastwards. Then, as his ears became more accustomed to the comparative silence, Huw heard from one side of the ditch and the other, the groans of the wounded and the dying.

It was both difficult and nauseating to extricate himself from under the already stiffening corporal. Huw pulled himself up the bank. Every square inch of him was plastered in mud, his Royal Navy uniform being totally unrecognisable. How much that mattered, he did not know. He had donned his uniform in the forlorn hope that, if he were captured, he would be treated properly as a prisoner of war in accordance with the Geneva Convention. However, he was well aware that the reality was that he would almost certainly be shot out of hand, either as a spy or as a commando. Surrender was definitely not one of his options. However, as he looked at the wounded men, each either struck by bullets or shrapnel, he realised that they, too, were so covered in mud that he was not conspicuously different from any of them. The down side of that was that, if he met up with the Poles, they would no doubt think him German. His navy blue uniform, even though covered in mud, might too readily be mistaken for the black of the Waffen SS and that would not endear him to any Polish soldier. There was a very real chance that they would shoot on sight.

Unsteadily, he knelt at the top of the bank. To the east, now at least a mile away, were the clouds of smoke and flashes of fire that told him that the battle-front was safely far from his present position. The uncertain fortunes of war, however, might mean that within minutes he could again be in the thick of it. A German soldier, clutching a profusely bleeding shoulder, shouted something but Huw could not make out what he was saying. He shrugged, waved to the man and rapidly crawled out of the other's sight. With any luck the fellow would think either that Huw was shell-shocked or that he had gone for help. He looked down at himself. Not only was he covered in mud, but the blood and brain-tissue of the corporal covered his upper torso. Anyone seeing him would think he was seriously wounded. A wave of nausea again swept over him. Fighting down the bile that surged to his throat, he rose to his feet and started a tottering run northwards towards the Scheldt. Once he reckoned he had put a safe distance between himself and the casualties in the ditch, he became more cautious. He rejoined the ditch and picked his way very slowly and carefully along it.

Once again, Huw's caution paid off.   From a short distance ahead, he began to hear muted voices and the sound of men moving furtively. He had no idea which side they were on, not that that seemed to matter much as he realised he was in as much danger from the one as the other. His only real hope was to get back to the safety of the barge. At least that would provide a roof over his head and there was still the prospect of warmth and some degree of comfort in the sleeping-bag he had left there. Out here in the open, if the soldiers of one side or the other did not get him, exposure all too soon would. He looked at his watch. Incredibly, it was scarcely five hours since he left the barge. The tide would be almost right out, making it impossible for him to reach the barge for at least another four hours, even if he were in a position to try. Somehow, he must evade capture and remain concealed, yet still be at the river bank in time to catch the last of the flood tide. There could be no question of waiting for darkness. With no light, he could not possibly find his way to the river bank, still less to the hole in the barge's side. Apart from that, the tide would be ebbing so strongly by then that he could not hope to swim against it. He simply had to get past whoever was ahead of him and reach the river bank and he had to do that within four hours.

Holding his breath, Huw eased himself up the side of the ditch, peering out through the reeds. Two hundred yards away, were three trucks under camouflage netting. Through the coarse mesh of the netting he could clearly see the black crosses that told him they were German. As he watched, men were unloading ammunition crates and small groups of soldiers were carrying these eastwards towards the front line. The vehicles had obviously come up river from Breskens but, in the absence of a bridge over the drainage ditch, were unable to go any nearer the action. The river, Huw reckoned, could be little more than a mile away to the north, but getting past the Germans undetected was going to be a major problem.

Knowing that the whole flat plain was drained by a series of herring-bone ditches, Huw made his way southwards away from the Germans and away from the river. After perhaps five hundred yards, he reached a point where smaller ditches from both east and west linked up with his. Going east would take him nearer the front line. Going west would bring him closer to the

German-held territory. In both cases, to reach the river to the north he would at some point have to cross the route being used by the Germans to re-supply their front line soldiers. Huw opted to go west. The problem was that he did not have a clue as to where the German main force might be. He could be safely several miles from it, or there might be heavily camouflaged troops only a matter of yards ahead.

Now he did not even crawl. He lay on his stomach and propelled himself with knees and elbows through the mud at the bottom of the ditch. This ditch he was now in was taking him south as well as west, farther and farther from the river. However, he dared not leave the cover it provided, or at least not until he was well clear of the ammunition trucks. Huw found it very difficult to estimate distance when moving so slowly and so clumsily. He glanced at his watch again. He had been moving for fifty minutes since leaving the main ditch - perhaps three hundred yards, he thought. He slid up the bank and parted the reeds carefully. The sun was now high in the sky and, for October, it was a warm and beautiful day. For a moment, as he looked out across the marshy meadow ahead, everything seemed peaceful, provided you ignored the rumble of battle somewhere far to the east.

Judging by the way the reeds followed a certain

line, there was another ditch a hundred yards away to the west, this one going in a north-westerly direction. That would take him back towards the river, but, at the same time, ever nearer German-held ground. Then there was the problem of crossing the open field between - a hundred yards with virtually no cover. Oh for a passing rain-squall! he thought, but there was no chance of that. Somewhere to the north there was the rumble of engines. The three trucks were returning along the track. Huw could not see them but a line of dust marked their course. Then, from much farther to the west, Huw saw an approaching cloud of dust. More trucks bringing more munitions were heading eastwards. Apart from perhaps providing a distraction for any bored forward sentry, none of this helped Huw. He would simply have to squirm his way over the open ground and hope for the best. For at least ten minutes he would be clearly visible if anyone was watching.

The trucks passed each other and Huw decided he would have to take the risk of crossing the open ground. Just as he was steeling his nerves to leave the comparative safety of the ditch, a new noise broke in upon him. In a rising crescendo, the roar of aircraft engines completely obliterated every other sound. From the west came four Spitfires, their RAF roundels clearly visible as they swooped down over the nearby line of laden trucks. There was the scream of rockets, the rattle of machine guns, then four columns of smoke from the ground. Guessing that any German in the vicinity would have his eyes fixed on the action to the north, Huw sprinted across the hundred yard gap, slithering into the welcoming mud of the other ditch in under fifteen seconds. He waited for shouts and shots, but none came. Reverting to his slow and cautious crawl, he slithered along the ditch until its north-westerly direction stopped at a deep drain with several feet of brackish water. It ran straight to the north and no doubt to the Scheldt. Now the problem was whether to follow the bank or to swim. Swimming seemed attractive, if only because it would wash away at least some of the stiff mud and gore from his uniform. However, he knew he must not be wet for too long. The day was deceptively warm, but it might be several hours before he could get out of his wet clothes. He chose to crawl along the bank on the western side, arguing that, if German eyes were looking eastward, they would be more likely to spot him if he were on the east bank.

In the distance to the east, the noise of battle was rising. Huw hoped that this was not because the Germans were in retreat and the front moving nearer him. He climbed the bank to look and realised that the increased noise was because the RAF were now joining the fray with a vengeance. Twin-engined aircraft, probably Mosquitoes, were making bombing runs and the Spitfires were diving and strafing. The risk now was that the German line might break dramatically and that the fighting sweep over the ground Huw had yet to traverse. Whilst, of course, he wanted an Allied victory, Huw desperately needed it to be delayed for an hour or more.

As he neared the track the German trucks had used, the smell of burning intensified. Then the light east wind brought whiffs of smoke. To his great delight, Huw found that, at the point he had to cross the track, there was a veritable smoke-screen. The cover it provided was very welcome, although there was a serious risk of stumbling into the enemy. Fearing the smoke might not last, Huw shambled forward at a crouch. If he met the Germans he would just have to hope that they would think he was one of their own injured. Certainly his blood-stained clothing would help give that impression. He scrambled up on to the track. Three or four men were just visible as vague shapes to his right. He swung round to the left and was swallowed up in the smoke either before he was noticed or before anyone thought there was something suspicious about him. A few yards farther on, he dropped off the track and down into a marshy piece of ground. He paused for breath as the acrid smoke caught at his throat. This dense smoke was too good to last. He had to put as much ground between himself and the track as he could before it cleared. Splashing through the marsh, he ran north until he fell into a shallow ditch. There, he lay flat until he got his breath back. The smoke was clearing and he could see several soldiers a mere hundred yards or so away on the road. As they were preoccupied with their wounded, they were not looking around them too much, so, meanwhile, Huw was safe.

From here on, he would have either to crawl or to squirm on his stomach. However, he was now past the track and, with any luck, there were no Germans between him and the Scheldt. Progress was slow, but Huw was unworried. He still had over two hours to reach the river and there was no great virtue in getting to its banks before the tide was high enough and slack enough for him to swim out. He did, in the event, reach the river with an hour to spare, which was just as well, for he was nearly half a mile downstream from the barge. The shore was thick with high reeds which gave him all the cover he needed as he made his way to a point opposite the hulk. After lying in the fading sun for half an hour until he was sure the tide was right, he slipped into the water and swam out to the wreck. He rounded the bows and duck-dived down into the murk, finding more by feel than by sight, the jagged opening in the hull. Gratefully, he pulled himself up into the chain-locker, glad to find that the water had almost washed his uniform clean

Huw peeled off the wet clothes, wrung them out as best he could and laid them out to dry, hoping that the residual warmth of that day's sun would take away most of the dampness. Then he crawled into his sleeping-bag, the only consolation being that he still had his meagre provisions which he eked out over the rest of the day.

That night, he hurriedly radioed England. SMFK was on duty, as always. Was SMFK one person or a team? he wondered, grateful that there was always this prompt response whenever he transmitted, day or night. Keeping his transmitting time as short as possible, partly to avoid detection and partly because of the state of 'Sleeping Beauty's' batteries, he transmitted 'V' - 'I require assistance' The reply came 'X' - 'Await my instructions.' Precious little help, that, thought Huw as he crawled, shivering, into his sleeping bag. When morning came he thought about getting up, but there was nothing to be done and, remembering some of the survival training advice for miners, should they be trapped below ground, he rested, conserving both heat and energy.

Chapter 10

As Huw lay dozing in his sleeping-bag, trying not to think of a bloated corpse that was stuck on the rusty coaming of the hold only a few feet from his head, a high-level conference was going on in Whitehall. The subject was Walcheron. Three weeks had gone by since the dike was breached and, whilst reconnaissance aircraft brought back ample evidence of the length of the gaps in the dikes, it was impossible to gauge the depth. The very worst thing that the Allied forces could do at this stage would be to send in landing craft packed with men and equipment if these might run aground right in front of the German shore batteries.

"Gentlemen," the same Admiral was in the chair as at the previous meeting when Huw had been given his assignment. "Gentlemen. We're in trouble at Walcheron. The RAF did a great job, but we still don't know if we can get our tanks and heavy equipment ashore. We do know the breaches in the dikes don't dry out at low tide, so there must be sufficient water at high tide for the small troop landing-craft. However, it would be sheer suicide to land lightly armed infantry unsupported by tanks and artillery. The problem is how to discover if there is enough water for tank landing craft.

"The Navy have made three reconnaissance sorties, trying to put surveying parties ashore. When the sea is calm, the Germans seem to be able to detect our chaps three or four miles out. We must assume their radar has improved. The last MTB was shelled and it was nothing short of miraculous that we didn't lose her. One party did get ashore and got some good information but, now that the Jerries will have guessed what we're up to, I don't thing we can get another party within a mile of the beach. Now that three weeks have gone by, it is impossible to guess what successive tides have done to the beaches. There may be entirely new sand-banks to contend with, for instance"

"Can the RAF not help here," asked the colonel. "I understand that the anti-aircraft guns are all out of action and the Germans have completely lost control of the air."

"We've some very encouraging air-photos, but we just cannot assess the depth of the water at the breaches in the dikes. Certainly, they do not dry out at low-tide, but they may only be a foot or two deep for all we know and, if we try to put troops ashore in insufficient water with no support from tanks, they'll be torn to shreds"

"Won't that happen anyway?" asked another army officer. "Attacking a coast so heavily defended with gun-emplacements is surely bound to be hazardous, to say the least. Have we any idea if the bombing reduced the number of batteries capable of action?"

"We hope it did, but are going on the pessimistic assumption that most will be still functioning as normal. I think it would be wrong to expect an easy victory. However, the RAF will pound the gun-batteries from the air all over again just before the landing-craft go in, whilst the Navy will pound them from the sea. We've allocated several capital ships for this. There are two reasons for this. The most obvious is that the heavy naval guns can do tremendous damage to the shore batteries. The second is that we think that, once these German guns are engaged by major units of the British Navy, they'll keep on returning fire and will ignore the small fry, by which I mean the landing-craft. The battle-cruisers and destroyers will certainly make a tempting target. And, of course, we'll screen the landing-craft with plenty of smoke. However, there's still the problem of the depth of water at the dikes."

"We had that fellow with the submersible canoe.

I gather he sent some good information. Can we not send him back?"

"Where is he now, Timpson?" asked the admiral.

"The poor devil's still stuck somewhere up the river. I gather he's out of food and practically out of power. He hasn't been able to reach the Canadians. Surrender is out of the question - the Jerries would put him up against a wall and shoot him as a spy. I rather fear he's had it, which is a great pity. He's done a great job and I'm confident that the invasion across the river at Flushing will go without a hitch, seeing he's given us the precise location of the mine-free corridor."

"Could he reconnoitre the dikes?"

"Perhaps. I know the man and I know that he'll try, but without food and possibly only able to operate on the surface using paddles, I wouldn't give much for his chances."

"When could he move?"

"At once, or, quite frankly, not at all. Without food, he'll die of exposure and heat-loss within days. We can contact him this evening and, if he can, he'll start tonight."

That settled it and, later on that evening, Huw received a long message with his instructions.

Chapter 11

Miserable with cold and with growing hunger pains, Huw prepared for his new assignment. He pumped air into the high-pressure bottles that allowed him to make the MSC dive or surface. His oxygen was all but exhausted so he would have to travel on the surface and dive only in extreme emergency. Even during the two minutes or so under water that were necessary to get 'Sleeping Beauty' clear of the barge, he could feel the batteries' strength tail off. However, the tide was ebbing and the night was dark. Navigating solely by compass, he paddled steadily downstream. He had eaten the last of his food thirty hours ago and it was hard to forget his hunger. Besides, he was growing light-headed and feeling the cold, both of which he knew to be symptoms of a low blood-sugar level. Added to that, the temperature in late-October was significantly lower than it had been when he arrived a month earlier. Even with every available stitch of clothing on, the cold soaked into his inner core.

It was not difficult to find the breach in the dike.

With the tide still ebbing, the water streaming through, it alerted him to its presence as it thrust him out to sea. Even if he had been at the peak of fitness, he would have had great difficulty fighting this current. In his half-starved and weakened state, he was powerless. Indeed, the current close in was altogether too strong for him to fight. Letting himself be swept out to sea by the current, he lay a mile or so off-shore waiting for the tide to change. When the tide slackened, he paddled in as fast as he could. He knew there would be an hour or two of slack water at low tide during which he could do his survey. After that, the in-coming tide would sweep him inland.

Stealthily, he approached the coast, hoping the German radar would not pick up his low form. With minimal battery power left, he did not have the option of running submerged. His luck held and, in the thin, grey light of dawn, he could just make out the dark shadow of the remaining section of the dike. To and fro he moved, from one end of the breach to the other, using his grapnel and mooring line to measure the depth as he did so. Eventually, as the rising tide strengthened, he could hold the MSC in the gap no longer. Neither could he paddle out to sea. He was left with no alternative but to allow himself to be carried inland on the flood tide. Once through the gap in the dike, Huw found that the current moderated. He was faced with flooded fields bounded to the west and the south by what was left of the dike. This looked more like a series of low-lying islands rather than a continuous sea-wall. As far as the eye could see in the dim light, to the north and east lay a vast inland-sea, strangely broken by the tops of buildings and trees. On its waters floated an immense assortment of debris. Huw was optimistic that his small craft would not be noticed among all this flotsam, at least until the light grew stronger. However, he had less than an hour in which to find some sort of shelter before full daylight. If he were still in open water after dawn and spotted by the enemy, there would simply be no where to run to.

As the sky was brightening by the minute from the east, Huw made out the top of a steeple rising out of the water. He paddled over and made fast alongside. Its upward slope was too steep to let him land on it, but he was able to drape the wireless aerial round it. Then he called up England, wondering as he did so, whether the feeble signal would be received.

SMFK was on the alert as usual. Huw transmitted his message as fast as he could. There was the ever-present risk of detection, although he felt reasonably certain that a wireless detection unit would be greatly hampered by the flooded roads. He ended his message with a brief statement that he was abandoning the MSC and would not be broadcasting again. With the usual 'received and understood' came an unofficial, 'would like to meet you when you get back.' This took him by surprise. He sent, 'when? where?' the message came back, 'Lyons, Strand. First of month 1800 hours.' 'Which month?' he sent. Reply: 'First you can manage.' Huw sent, 'OK, over and out.' Then he gratefully switched off.

Huw paddled away, strangely encouraged. SMFK thought he would come through alive. Indeed, he felt positively elated that someone in England thought he had even the slimmest chance. Now he must get away from the coast and find a hiding place before he was spotted in the growing light. A mile or so to the east, the roofs of a small group of buildings were sticking a few feet out of the water. He paddled over as fast as his dwindling reserves of strength would permit. This really was his only hope. He must find shelter here. He had neither the time nor the strength to press on any farther.

The buildings must have been a small farm. A single-storey farm-house was so low-lying that only the ridge of the roof broke the surface. Slightly more of another two buildings were visible. These looked promising. The roofs were in good repair, having only the occasional broken tile. However, there was no way of getting into them from above water, short of tearing off the tiles. Huw carefully adjusted his air supply and took 'Sleeping Beauty' down gently. It was pitch dark between the buildings twenty feet below the surface but, by the feeble light of his failing torch, he made his way into one of them. Swimming carefully upwards, he broke the surface almost at the level of the roof timbers inside a barn. To his great relief, he saw in the half-light that penetrated through the broken tiles that there was a hay-loft just above the water-level at one end. A few strokes and he was there. He pulled himself up and lay, panting, on the worm-eaten timber. He pulled off his helmet and gratefully sucked in the musty, malodorous air.

As the sun rose, so a little more light penetrated through crannies in the tiles above him and, as the day wore on, the temperature increased. The straw was not wet, although everything felt somewhat damp. He stripped off most of his clothes, suddenly conscious of how long it was since he had been able to wash or shave. He made a deep nest for himself in the straw and fell sound asleep.

Early in the afternoon, Huw woke up. The sun had heated the space under the tiles and, for the first time in days, he felt really warm. However, his first conscious thought was about food. Hunger was the dominant feeling and all the other comforts and discomforts of his situation seemed to pale into insignificance beside this. Suddenly he realised there was food to be had. Nothing special, but, in the circumstances, very welcome. The straw on which he had been lying had been threshed, but with something less than one hundred percent efficiency. Here and there was a grain of wheat. On the floor of the hay-loft under the straw was a mixture of dust and wheat grain. Between the rough planks that made up the floor were still more. Huw scraped some up and blew off the dust. The resulting grain still looked dirty but, once rinsed with some of his precious supply of water, it looked reasonably clean. Whatever its nutritional value, he felt much better when he had chewed three or four mouthfuls.

In the late afternoon, the light dimmed and Huw realised the sky was becoming overcast. Soon he heard the patter of rain on the tiles above him, first a gentle shower, then a down-pour. Quickly, he went to work on one tile that looked slightly insecure. In a matter of minutes he had the tile pushed aside and a steady trickle of reasonably clean water streamed in. Gratefully, he caught it in his water bottle.

The rain continued into the evening and Huw decided he would remain in this barn for another night and day. He knew he was uncomfortably near the coast and might well be caught up in the inevitable bombing and shelling that would precede an invasion. However, he felt confident that the Allies would not have been able to react so quickly to his last report as to be in a position to invade within a day of receiving it.

As he watched the rainwater streaming through the small hole he had made in the roof, the sight of so much clean water made him long for a really good wash. Perhaps he could find something to collect enough water in. He donned his diving suit, picked up his torch and swam down into the depths of the barn below. The chances of finding food in the submerged farmhouse seemed practically negligible. Only canned food could have survived and still be edible. However, Huw knew that the Dutch had already suffered great shortages and therefore the chances of finding food lying in the larder were poor. However, it was worth trying, so he swam over to the farmhouse.

The occupants had obviously left in a hurry as the sea-waters had risen. The door was still ajar, so Huw, using his torch, picked his way in. Most of the furniture was made of wood and naturally had floated to the ceiling so, ducking under the legs of chairs and tables, he headed towards the rear of the building where he rightly assumed the kitchen would be. A kitchen stool was visible, floating at ceiling height, but everything else - crockery, pots, pans and various utensils - were still tidily placed on shelves, albeit covered with a fine slime. Beside the sink was a milking pail. Huw picked it up and placed in it a large mixing bowl. He then eased open a cupboard door and found himself looking into a larder. There had obviously been very little food and most of that was now an unrecognisable pulpy mass. However, there was a large, rather rotten looking turnip. Huw put it in the pail. Behind it was another round lump rather larger than a cricket ball. He could not identify it, but put it in the pail too. In a small basin were five eggs. Carefully, he picked them up. Each was coated with a green scum. He had no idea if the filthy water would have penetrated the shells, but it would be worth trying them.

There was nothing else worth taking and, conscious of his dwindling air supply, Huw hurried back to the barn and was soon sitting in the hay-loft examining his finds.

The pail he set in place to catch the rain-water. The eggs were intact and, after carefully washing the shells, Huw broke and ate three of them raw. The turnip was rotten, but there was still some edible parts near the heart of it. He hacked away the rotten bits and chewed gratefully on what was left. The smaller spherical lump turned out to be a cheese. It was protected by a thick layer of wax and a heavy rind and the cheese inside was perfect. After eating half of it, Huw really started to feel better. The rest of the evening was spent washing first himself, then his clothes. The steady down-pour outside provided all the water he needed. He spread his clothes out to dry. Fortunately, despite the rain, it was still tolerably warm in the loft so, practically naked, he continued the pains-taking task of retrieving grains of wheat. Some he ate and the rest he left steeping in a bowl of water overnight in the hope that they would be more palatable the next day.

Chapter 12

Warm in the straw, Huw slept more soundly that night than he had at any time since his arrival in Holland. When he woke, it was already broad-daylight. The rain had stopped and thin rays of sun-light penetrated through the occasional crack between the tiles. The temperature was rising and, for October, it looked like being an unusually warm day. Huw knew he ought to move east-wards away from the breached dike. The attack on Walcheron would not be long delayed and, if he did not put a few more miles between himself and the main action, there was a serious risk of being bombed or shelled by his own side. However, movement was impossible in daylight.

About noon, Huw swam out of the barn and up to the surface. He felt reasonably safe as he came up between the buildings because they would screen him from German eyes. However, they would also prevent him seeing very much. He looked round and saw the top of a large sycamore tree which, though it had lost most of its foliage, still had sufficient autumnally tinted leaves left to conceal him. He climbed into its branches and looked round.

To the west, he could see the church-spire from where he had sent his final wireless message and, beyond it across the flooded fields, the broken line of the dike and the rear of several shore-batteries. On the other three sides, there was mainly water, with the occasional tree, roof or the top of a wind-mill sticking up skywards. It was a beautiful day, with the sun glinting on the water, practically no wind and each tree or building reflected in the millpond-like flood-water. Far to the south, he could see a small barge with soldiers packed on it, crossing the flood-water, heading for the distant dike. With some satisfaction, he thought how difficult it must be for the Germans to keep their defence lines supplied and manned now that all the roads were cut. However, he thought, too, of how difficult the coming Allied invasion would be. The importance of the landing-craft getting through the dikes, not just for the first assault, but to push the enemy back, struck him as never before. Despite the problem of the presence of the heavy guns guarding the coast, the Allies would just have to get tank landing-craft through to provide the support of amphibious tanks and lorries for the infantry. A bloody battle lay ahead to be fought and won on and around the beaches and dikes to the west. However, that would be only the start. The

Germans would have to be pushed back eastwards and nothwards until not only was Walcheron free but also the whole of the south of Holland. Then, and only then, could the vital port of Antwerp be brought into use. Until that day, all supplies and reinforcements for the troops who landed from the sea to retake the south and west of Walcheron would have to be brought in through the all-important breaches in the dikes.

Huw's own immediate problem was where to move to. Move he must, but he could not do so in daylight. However, moving at night would bring the enormous risk of blundering into Germans in the dark. After such a beautiful day, the sky would be clear that night. However, there would be no moon. This was a mixed blessing. The darkness would cover his own movements, but it would make navigation extremely difficult.

Over to the north-east, Huw spotted a steeple, or rather, the top of one, sticking out of the water some five miles away. There was no sign of an accompanying church or, indeed, of any other building. Apart from the tips of a few trees, the steeple stood alone. That could only mean that the water must be particularly deep there. It was highly unlikely that the steeple stood by itself, so Huw assumed that the church that went with it must be entirely submerged. In other words, the water would be thirty to forty feet in depth. If he could get into the steeple under water, he might find a secure hide-out among the bells and be relatively safe. Very carefully, he took a compass-bearing on it. Finding such a small target in the dark would be tricky, to say the least, so he also took bearings on what looked like two pieces of high ground to the east. These were almost certainly very much in German hands. However, he would have to take his chances landing there, should the steeple prove uninhabitable or if he failed to find it in the dark.

As soon as it was dark, Huw stowed his few possessions in a water-tight container and swam down to where 'Sleeping Beauty' lay outside the barn. He had eaten the remaining eggs and most of the cheese. All he now had was the small amount of cheese left and about a couple of pounds or so of wheat. Eating the uncooked grains provided a comforting illusion of having fed, but he doubted whether it really nourished him at all. Finding a safe hiding place where he could sit out the coming invasion was top priority, but finding food came a close second.

'Sleeping Beauty' broke the surface in nearly total darkness. Huw did not even try to use her motor. If any power was left, it was better to conserve it in case, in an emergency, he needed to move submerged. Silently, he paddled away from the farm, keeping strictly to his compass bearing. As his eyes became more accustomed to the dark, Huw was surprised how much he could see by star-light. This could cause problems, of course. If he could see, he could be seen. However, he had no real choice but to take the risk. The one consolation was that this part of the island must have been particularly low-lying. There were very few trees or buildings showing above the surface and therefore it was unlikely that there were any German units in the area.

The night was still and silent. Apart from the slight splash of his own paddles, the ripple of the water past the boat's hull and the occasional cry of a nocturnal bird, a complete hush covered the waters. Then, across the water, Huw heard the distant, muted sound of a boat's engine. It grew steadily louder, so he paddled gently into the shelter of a tree. Quietly, he let air out of the ballast tanks and 'Sleeping Beauty' gently subsided below the surface until only Huw's head remained above it. Straining his eyes, he could just make out some kind of small fishing boat and the coal-scuttle helmets of half a dozen or so German soldiers. Had they detected his presence? Were they actively searching for him, or was this just a coincidence? He pulled on his helmet and prepared to submerge. Under water he would be reasonably safe, but his oxygen supply was all but done. Furthermore, if they really suspected he was there and started tossing grenades in, he did not like to think of the effect of an underwater explosion on the human body.

The boat passed a mere fifty yards from Huw, but it did pass. His presence had not even been suspected and he assumed that this was either a random patrol or a change of guard going to relieve some pill-box on the sea-facing dike. The wake of the other craft splashed gently into Huw's face. When the sound of the motor had all but tailed off, Huw brought the MSC to the surface and continued on his cautious way. His navigation was good and he started to make out the dark mass of the steeple against the Milky Way above. Fully twenty feet of the tower protruded above the surface. There were no windows or openings at the water level but eight feet up were the wooden louvers that told Huw that this was, indeed, a bell-tower. Above water, there was no way of getting in. Much now depended on whether, like English churches, their Dutch counterparts were left unlocked to allow access for private worship. Huw adjusted his air-supply, then let 'Sleeping Beauty' sink gently down close to the steeple wall. The darkness below the water was absolute and Huw's weakening torch made little impression on the blackness. However, as the MSC bottomed, he slid out of the cockpit and, partly by torch-light but more by groping, he found a door. It was indeed unlocked. The darkness inside was, if that were possible, even more oppressive. Shining his feeble light round, he saw another door ahead. He pushed it open. A cavern of darkness faced him, his feeble torch making virtually no impression. Then he made out the back of a pew. He was in the church itself. He withdrew into the vestibule area and hunted round. A small door gave off to the right. It opened with some difficulty and Huw formed the opinion that its hinges were rusted with lack of use. Before him was a small space and a ladder leading almost vertically up the tower.

Huw let himself float upwards. He passed through a hatch and found himself in a small room. Shining his torch up, he saw bells-ropes curling like weird snakes, neutrally buoyant in the water. Behind him was another ladder. Pulling on a rung, he continued his ascent. Another hatchway, another floor, another vertical ladder. Again he went up and, this time, he broke surface after about five feet. The ladder stretched upwards to a third hatch seven feet higher. Huw climbed through it and found himself on a narrow staging which encircled bells of varying sizes. There was little room on the walk-way, but still just sufficient for him to make a reasonable lodging for himself. He descended and, with some difficulty, returned aloft with the water-tight container. With still a couple of hours until dawn and a constant need to use the battery of his torch as little as possible, Huw pulled out his sleeping bag and huddled himself in a corner, trying to doze before sunrise would enable him to get himself better organised.

Chapter 13

Rather surprisingly Huw did sleep, but he was suddenly shaken into wakefulness by a colossal explosion. It was still dark and he was confused and disorientated. The explosion of noise went on and on and on, like some interminable roll of thunder. The brickwork of the tower vibrated and an eerie harmonic ring came from the bells. Huw pulled himself erect and peered out through the louvers. The whole of the sky to the west was lit up with a seemingly unbroken series of explosions. Overhead, three Mosquitoes circled, dropping flares over the western sea-dike. Far out to sea was the smoke and the flashes of heavy guns being fired by what was obviously a considerable fleet. The Mosquitoes suddenly swooped in his direction and, behind them he saw wave after wave of heavy, four-engined bombers, bomb-doors open, flying eastwards over the dikes. Being six or so miles away, he could not see the bombs fall, but he could see the result. For a brief moment, Huw pitied the German soldiers manning the coastal defences. The noise was thunderous even at this distance. What it would be like at the receiving end of such an onslaught, he could scarcely imagine.

There was action, too, to the south of him. This time, it was not so dramatic, but dark clouds of smoke rolled over the flat landscape. Huw realised that he must be somewhere north-east of Flushing. The Allies would be crossing the narrow stretch of the River Scheldt, using the mine-free corridor he had identified. To save risk to Dutch lives, instead of using high-explosive, they must be shelling the whole place with smoke-bombs to cover their crossing and landing.

For an hour and a half the bedlam continued. Then, as suddenly as they had started, the noise of the guns diminished and the skies cleared of bombers. The naval bombardment had stopped but the German guns that were still operational continued to fire, albeit rather raggedly. Clearly, the landing craft were closing with the shore. The dunes and the dike were now shrouded in smoke. The crackle of smaller calibre weapons could now be heard faintly between the German salvoes. Using his binoculars, Huw watched small landing craft emerging through the smoke, fanning out, then turning and disappearing into the smoke once more. As the day went on, the smoke began to clear and he could see troops, at this range looking like ants even when viewed through the glasses, swarming along the shore. He was too far away to see the tracer bullets from machine-guns, but he did see the flash of fire as flame-throwers poured their deadly liquid fire into pill-boxes, gun-emplacements and trenches. Beyond the dike, four separate columns of smoke rose skyward. Huw feared that this indicated that the attackers had not had an easy, unopposed landing and that men were still fighting and dying in stranded tank-landing craft.

Nearer at hand, a flotilla of boats, each packed with German soldiers chugged towards the scene of the action. Then, out of the skies screamed Spitfires. One after another, machine-guns chattering death, they swooped over the boats until not a single one was left afloat. All that was left was a little debris floating on the surface. So far as Huw could determine, there were no survivors. No doubt the heavily armed Germans had been pulled under by the sheer weight of their own kit. A dramatic illustration of the importance of having mastery of the skies, thought Huw. Indeed, throughout the whole of that long day, he did not see a single German aircraft.

Early in the afternoon, the sound of gunfire came with increasing ferocity from the east. The Allies were evidently attacking Walcheron from mainland Holland as well as from the south and the west. The battle might be long and much more blood yet be shed, but of the eventual outcome, there could be no doubt. That, indeed, reflected, Huw, was true of the whole war in Europe. Germany was beset on all sides by vastly superior forces. How many needless deaths must there be, he wondered, just because one man in Berlin could not face facts?

On his man-made island refuge, Huw had a grandstand view. Not that he saw very much. The progress of the battle, or rather, battles, was more perceived by noting puffs of smoke from distant guns and mortars, rather than actually seeing the advance of the Allied troops, more by hearing than by observing the development of the struggle. However, towards evening, the noise of battle began to abate. On a distant dike to the south, he saw a long column of German troops, their hands high above their heads, being escorted eastwards by Allied soldiers. Amphibious tanks and DUWKs manoeuvred across the flooded fields to the south-west. The forces who landed at Flushing had linked up with the main invasion forces and the amphibious lorries were re-equipping them for the next day's mopping up work.

Huw ate the last of his food. He must now try to reach Allied lines without falling foul of retreating German units on the one hand, nor being shot by a trigger happy Tommy on the other.

Chapter 14

At twilight, Huw made his way down to 'Sleeping Beauty'. Although he felt that, by this time tomorrow, he would have reached the safety of Allied lines or be dead, he still packed the water-tight container. For nearly an hour he paddled steadily eastward, moving slowly so as to minimise the ripples he caused. As he approached as quietly as he could the higher ground ahead of him, he heard movement in the bushes on the bank. He froze. Then came more furtive sounds and then, for a brief moment, he saw a coal-scuttle helmet, then another. Huw shuddered. He had stumbled into a party of retreating Germans. Silently, he submerged the boat, until only his head was above the water. Growing colder by the minute, he remained stationary until the last sound had died away. He resurfaced and backed the MSC away. From his left came distant shouts, the bang of a grenade and the crackle of gun-fire. This was not the right place to land. Hurriedly he retreated, first westwards, then south.

An hour, and four miles later, Huw turned

eastwards again, letting the craft approach the land at about one mile an hour. It beached silently. For long minutes he sat stock-still, listening. He heard nothing and so, backing off into deeper water, he submerged 'Sleeping Beauty' for what he hoped would be the last time. He patted her cock-pit coaming affectionately, but a streak of pessimism led him to wade ashore with a mooring rope which he trailed out, concealing it in the grass, and finally tying it to a bush. He peeled of his diving gear and stowed it out of sight. Finally, high on the bush, he fastened a piece of white cloth. With any luck, he could find the MSC, should he need her again.

Very cautiously, Huw worked his way up the rising ground. Over a slight crest, he could hear the sounds of men. He lay still, prostrate in the wet grass. The noises came from a wide area ahead of him and, although he could not see it, he sensed that there was a considerable encampment within the next few hundred yards. Crawling very carefully, he closed the gap. Now he could smell the tantalising odours of wood-smoke and cooking. He was sure that he caught an occasional word in English, but how to make contact without collecting a bullet from a nervous sentry was now his problem. He was just wondering how to proceed, when he heard an rustle fairly close by. Then there came a different sound, which for a second he could not identify.

Suddenly, he realised someone was singing almost under his breath only a few yards away. The tune was familiar. Then he could make out the words:

'Noddfa arall, gwn, nid oes,
Ond tydi, i'm henaid gwann;
Ti fu farw ar y Groes,
Yw fy nghymorth ym mhob man;'

Welsh! Now who the blazes was singing in Welsh in the middle of a battle in the Netherlands? As the voice went on:

'Ynot ti, fi Iesu, mae
Holl ymddiried f'enaid byw;'

Huw joined in softly. The other stopped abruptly and Huw sung on alone:

'Nerth rho imi i barhau
Nes dod adref at fy Nuw.'

Then there was a silence, broken by a voice in Welsh, "Who's there?"

"Another lad from the Valleys," replied Huw, also in Welsh. "Where are you from, Treorchy? I can't quite place the accent, but you're from Rhondda and that's a fact."

"Close! Tonypandy in fact, but eleven years in Canada has perhaps blurred it a bit. Who are you?"

"Huw Morgan, Lieutenant, Royal Navy. And you?"

"Royal Navy? You're a bit off course, aren't you? Step forward slowly and let's have a look at you."

Huw moved out into the open, his hands at shoulder height. In the dim light, he saw a tall figure with a sten-gun at the ready. The man was clearly both nervous and suspicious, so he sought to put his mind at ease.

"So what's a lad from the Valley's doing with the Canadian lot?" he asked.

"My dad didn't want me going down the pits, so when things got really bad during the slump, he took us all to Canada. He was so pleased when I was accepted in the army! 'Ceremonial only,' he said. 'I can't see the Canadians ever going to war. Their only neighbour is the States, so there's no-one else for them to fall out with. You'll be safer there than in a civilian job!' That's what he thought! We've been advancing waist-deep in freezing water and crawling through ditches which are mud-baths, being shot at on every side. Where did you learn to sing like that?"

"Chapel. Primitive Methodist Sunday School in Cwmparc. Mostly Wesley's hymns. In fact, I can't remember any others. I haven't heard that one for years. When I heard you singing, 'Cover my defenceless head with the shadow of Thy wings' it seemed to sum up all my own thoughts. Who are you, by the way?"

"Davies. Evan Davies, Captain, Canadian 2nd Division. Well, I'd better take you to the colonel. Keep your hands up. Our lads are a bit quick on the draw, you might say."

The two moved forward, still chatting in Welsh about the Rhondda valley and schooldays there. They reached the camp and, feeling not unlike a prisoner of war, Huw was escorted past bivouacs erected alongside tanks and lorries. Tired men either smoked or dozed. Some looked at him with mild interest but most seemed too tired to pay much attention. Soon he was relating his story to a very suspicious Canadian colonel. The man seemed less than satisfied and Huw was told he would be taken, still under guard, to a field kitchen and fed whilst the colonel tried to contact the intelligence service in Antwerp. As he moved off, he heard the colonel say to the Welsh soldier. "Are you sure he's kosher, Davies? These Jerries are a devious lot, you know."

"Well," came the reply accompanied by a broad smile, "it did occur to me that he might possibly be a Welsh-speaking Kraut who happened to be a Primitive Methodist sent to spy on us, but I thought you'd like to give him a hearing so I didn't shoot him!"

"So his Welsh is good, then?"

"The real thing, trust me. The accent and the slang would be nearly impossible for an impostor to get right. Apart from that, he obviously knows the Welsh mining valleys too well for mere book-learning. Anyway, the intelligence boys'll soon sort him out."

They did. Before the unit was ready to move out the next day, signals had been exchanged with London. The recognition words that Huw had been given before leaving England were sent and approved.

"Your chap's kosher, all right, Davies. Seems the Brits think pretty highly of him. He's to get VIP treatment. We've to get him to Antwerp tonight. A Dakota'll be waiting there to take him back to England. Make sure he's got everything he needs. Oh! And by the way, it's perhaps as well you didn't shoot first and ask questions later!"

Chapter 15

It was only when he was back on English soil that Huw thought about his own health. The weeks of being more in his diving suit than out of it, added to his generally run-down condition caused by poor diet, not to say near-starvation, had brought him out in a series of salt-water boils. Various minor cuts and scrapes acquired over the last month had refused to heal and were now turning septic. After a short debriefing session he was hospitalised and treated with the new wonder drug called penicillin. Rapidly he returned to normal strength and then, late in November, he was once more posted to the Shetlands. He was now something of a celebrity in the exclusive club of diver-pilots of MSCs and certainly had more field experience than did any of his colleagues. It was quite natural, therefore, that he was ordered to act as leading instructor. All the training now was in preparation for an attack on the new German 'super U-boats' that were operating with devastating effect out of the Norwegian fjords.

December was half gone before Huw

remembered his tryst with SMFK. Remembering the fillip this proposed rendezvous had been to his morale at one of the loneliest moments of his life, Huw felt quite guilty. However, he could do nothing to communicate with SMFK who, no doubt, was now the opposite number of some other lonely soul behind enemy lines. In all probability, SMFK would have forgotten him weeks ago anyway.

It was a big disappointment that Huw did not get leave at Christmas. It was months since he had visited his widowed mother in Wales. However, the war could not stop for the festive season and, if Huw celebrated Christmas at all, it was twenty feet below Scapa Flow, sneaking up on a cruiser whose crew, despite the celebrations, were supposed to be at full readiness. However he did get two weeks leave when the lucky ones who had spent Christmas with their families returned.

On the afternoon of the first of January, Huw walked along the Strand. Lyon's Cornerhouse was open for business as usual despite being somewhat scarred by bomb fragments. Picking his way past sandbags, Huw entered. It was packed with customers, most in uniform of one kind or another. He felt rather foolish. How was he to make contact with someone he did not know at all among so many people? He stepped back outside and walked on, passing the depressingly large number of bombed out buildings on both sides of the road until he reached St Paul's Cathedral. It, too, was open for business and he went and sat inside in silent meditation.

Memories of boyhood and of the little chapel in the Rhondda flooded back. He really should be here giving thanks. He knew that, but somehow he found it difficult to pray. Not for the first time in recent days, he found himself thinking of Tennyson's lines from 'The Passing of Arthur': *More things are wrought by prayer than this world dreams of.*

Back at Cwmparc his mother would not have let a day go by without pleading with her God for her son. With a blush, he recalled the day when she had quoted Tennyson's 'The Passing of Arthur' very aptly back to him.

"For what are men better than sheep or goats
That nourish a blind life within the brain,
If, knowing God, they lift not hands of prayer
Both for themselves and those who call them friend?"

Yes, he knew he ought to pray, but still he could not. The harsh realities of war made all that he had been taught about a God of Love seem remote and, to his war-weary mind, nearly beyond belief. However, there was a peace in that place of worship and, although he had not prayed, he eventually came out into the cold of the winter evening feeling at least more composed and at rest about the future.

At ten minutes to six, he entered the restaurant and ordered coffee. It was not quite so crowded as it had been earlier and he found a table near the door. He pulled a large envelope out of his pocket and wrote in large letters, 'PGRB'. He placed it prominently in front of him. Several men and women went by, some in civvies, most in uniform. One or two glanced at it and at him, but no one spoke. Just after six, a voice at his elbow said, "Do you mind if I share your table?"

Huw looked up and saw a pair of eyes so dark that they seemed almost black, set in a coffee-brown face that was framed with jet black hair. The place was crowded certainly, but if the girl bothered to look, surely she could find somewhere else to look. Hiding his annoyance, he waved to the empty chair opposite, trying by his silence to make clear at the same time that he wanted no conversation with a stranger. Several more men and women passed the table, but the girl's luxuriant head of hair was probably hiding his notice. He glanced at his watch - ten past. He could hardly spin out his coffee any longer. Should he order more or just go? Impulsively, he picked up his spoon and tapped the side of the cup. 'PGRB PGRB' twice in quick succession. Silly, really, he thought. The tinkling sound was barely audible over the murmur of conversation. He reached for his kit-bag but as he did so the girl opposite, without looking up, tapped gently on the table, 'SMFK SMFK.'

Huw sat down again and his jaw literally dropped. Could this girl, and girl indeed she looked, for she did not seem a day over eighteen, really be the vital link that had kept him in touch with England?

"SMFK?" he asked, incredulously.

"PGRB, I presume," she replied with a shy smile. "I know I'm not what you expected, but I hope you don't mind"

"Mind?" Huw asked. "Why ever should I? Of course, I had no idea who you were and, no doubt, you had no idea what I looked like."

"Well, it was easier for me. I knew you would almost certainly not be a woman. You had to be young to endure all you have. You're in Navy uniform, which further narrowed the field. So I knew it was you before I even sat down."

"Then why the devil didn't you tell me? You sat there for ten minutes while I was getting more and more certain no one was coming. Why?"

"Times are changing, but it's still not every Englishman that will share a table with someone with brown skin. If you had obviously been embarrassed at my company, I would have slipped away again."

Hiding his confusion, Huw muttered, "I'm not English. I'm Welsh"

"Ah!" she replied with a grin, "From another of England's oppressed colonies, are you?"

"You could put it like that! Anyway! I'm glad you're here. Let's have something to eat. Are you hungry? Oh! By the way, I can hardly call you SMFK all evening. I'm Huw Morgan. What's your name?"

"Zara Khan," she replied.

Chapter 16

Autumn 1996, an ice-house near Port Appin.

Day-dreaming about the past helped Huw Morgan to cope with the discomforts of the present. Going over the events that had led to that first meeting with the girl he would marry was of some use as he lay trussed like a chicken he knew not where. However, he was dragged out of the past by the sound of movement somewhere in the blackness behind him. 'Rats!' he thought. 'That's all I need.' In the best books, they would nibble through the ropes that bound him. With his luck, they would start eating him without having the decency to wait for him to die!

Then the rustle became a series of grunts. The old, familiar Morse! PGRB PGRB, followed by W - the international code for 'I require medical assistance.'

Huw grunted a reply, almost choking on his gag as he did so. The bitter disappointment that Zara, too, had been captured sank in. Now there was no hope of the cavalry arriving in the nick of time. They were together.

They would die together. Although they had never discussed the matter, Huw knew that Zara would be no more interested in out-living him than he did of out-living her. As doctors, they both knew the score. Neither had long to go. Huw was well aware of that, but anger surged through him that the pair of them should end up the victims of the tribal warfare that had brought so much misery to the Island of Ireland.

The two were wriggling along the uneven floor until their bodies touched. Huw signalled. 'Lighter. Left pocket.'

Zara, still lithe despite her age and painfully thin because of her illness, drew her knees up to her chest and, having managed to kick off her shoes, passed her feet over the ropes that had bound her wrists behind her back. With her hands still tied, she groped in her husband's anorak pocket. Thinking ruefully of the number of times she had nagged him to give up pipe-smoking, she pulled out the lighter and a dazzling flame seemed to light the darkness like a flare. Propping the lighter up, Zara went to work on the ropes that tied her husband's wrists. After a few nail-tearing minutes, his hands were free and he soon had her untied. Then he released his feet and, picking up the lighter, he looked round their prison. It was about twenty feet wide. How far it went back was impossible to guess, certainly much farther than the circle of light cast by his lighter. The roof was curved like the underside of a bridge and was made of large, unhewn stones that looked as though they had been dredged from a river-bed. The door, which was set in a wall of equally massive construction, was of heavy timber and such a precise fit that it was almost impossible to guess if it was daylight outside. He turned round. Before him, in an untidy pile sloping up to the vaulted ceiling, was a chaotic assortment of lobster-pots, marker buoys and fishing-nets. Small wonder the place stank!

"The old ice-house!" he said. "We're in the old ice-house."

The old building, dating back to pre-refrigeration days, was set into the dunes. Little more than its front wall protruded from the marran-grass covered sand behind it. She vaguely knew that the fishing folk of last century packed such buildings with ice in the winter and, because of the insulating effect of thick walls and several feet of sand or earth on top, the ice remained there for months without thawing, keeping their catches of fish fresh throughout the following summer. The exceptionally thick, close-fitting door was not for security, but for insulation.

There was no point in exploring among the fishing nets for a back door. There would not be one.

Further examination of the one and only exit from their prison convinced them that they were hopelessly stuck there.

"Now what?" asked Huw. "If I were younger, we might just have a chance of taking them by surprise when they come back, but not now."

"*If* they come back, you mean."

"No! They'll be back. This place is used by some fisherman and they daren't take the risk of him finding us before they've done their business. McPhee doesn't seem to have recognised us, at least, not yet. If he does and realises we could identify him, then that would be that. Even if he doesn't, we'll have to face the fact that they can't leave us here and they can't let us go." He looked at his watch. "Half past five. It must be nearly daylight outside. My guess is that they will come for us very soon now."

"To kill us?"

"No, not yet at least. If they were going to do that, they would have done so right away. My guess is that they'll take us somewhere else well away from here. I can't see them just releasing us, so it doesn't look good, I'm afraid."

"Can we not make some kind of a fight of it? I know there's no realistic chance of beating them, but we might take at least one with us. I hate the idea of just waiting for them to come and finish us off." Zara looked round for anything which might be used as a weapon.

"I don't think they dare kill us here. What with the Irishmen in the hotel at Oban, then perhaps someone may have seen the boat in the bay, and add to that Ireland not too far away, there'd be too much risk of the police making the connection. No! I think they'll take us with them, at least part of the way."

"Part of the way where?"

"London would be my guess. I managed to open one of those canisters before I was caught. If I'm not mistaken, it's packed with home-made explosive. You know, the stuff the IRA make from fertiliser. There's also boxes which look as though they may contain guns and ammunition. I think our friends are planning a dramatic interruption of the talks on the future of Ireland that there's been all the stuff about in the papers. You know. All the key players are meeting at Downing Street later this week."

"So they'll take us with them, you think?"

"Yes, no doubt dropping us off in a shallow grave somewhere well away from here." Huw replied with brutal realism.

"So, what do we do?"

"I think we'll have to hope for a chance to hit back somewhere, but not here. There's no hope of beating two or more of these thugs in a straight fight, even with the advantage of surprise. We'll tie ourselves up again, but this time in a way that we can release the ropes easily. We'll put the gags round our faces but leave out the bit that was stuck in our mouths. That way, we can easily push them off when we want to. After that, we'll just have to play it by ear."

As he tied her up, Zara told Huw what had happened to her. She had retreated to the ice-house and was awaiting his signal. Time drifted by and, just as she was getting really worried, she heard footsteps on the path. In the darkness she saw two men approach, one with a heavy load over his shoulder. Knowing she would be spotted as they went passed, Zara had tried to withdraw farther into the scrub behind the ice-house. However, she had been spotted and, like her husband, slugged down from behind.

Huw tied the rope firmly round one of Zara's wrists, then coiled it several times round the other until, at a superficial glance, it looked as though both hands were tightly bound to each other. He did the same with the feet. Finally, having tied Zara hand and foot in this way and then tied his own feet, he did the same with his own hands, winding the rope round his free wrist until his hands were about a foot apart. He then sat down and passed his feet over the rope so that his hands were behind him once more. With three more turns of his wrist, he had wound up all the slack and he looked helplessly tied up once more. Now all they could do was to wait. As before, Huw sought to detach himself from the present discomforts by drifting back in time.

Chapter 17

London 1945

After his first meeting with Zara in the Lyons Cornerhouse, Huw met her several times during the brief spell of leave. On his return to Scapa Flow, the two continued to correspond. The war in Europe was drawing to its inevitable close and the attack on the U-boats was cancelled. In May came the great celebration of victory in Europe, but, for Huw, the occasion was clouded by the certainty that he would be posted to the Far East where the war with Japan continued with ever greater ferocity on both sides. After six years, Huw was war-weary. He had survived thus far, but the Far East was a harsh theatre of war. The Motor Submersible Canoes had been used with encouraging results against Japanese shipping but the combination of an utterly ruthless enemy and the shark-infested waters meant the cost in lives was awful. The coming of Zara into his life had given him a tremendous desire to survive, but his natural pessimism prevented him even discussing the future with her, let alone proposing marriage which was what he really wished.

In late June and early July, they met when he was on embarkation leave and spent every available minute together. However, the shadows of war hung over them both and all their happiness was tinged with sorrow. In mid-July, Huw reported to Portsmouth and, after some delay, the naval auxiliary on which he, his colleagues and a total of twelve MSCs were to travel, put to sea. After an uncomfortable crossing of the Bay of Biscay, the ship passed Gibraltar in the late evening of a hot summer's day. It seemed strange to see the base all lit up after so many years of black-out and the bright lights brought home to him that the war in Europe was at last just a bad memory from the past. The future, in Japanese waters, was all too real however. It was in this spirit of pessimism that Huw watched the Mediterranean slip by. The ship passed through the Suez Canal and was crossing the Indian Ocean when, waking one morning, Huw realised that, at some time during the night, they had change course. The rising sun which should have been over the bows was over the stern. Puzzled, he strode along the deck. A strange excitement seemed to have gripped the officers who he saw talking on the bridge above him.

One of them leaned over the rail and called down

to him, "It's over! The Nips have thrown in the towel! Sparks got it on the radio and we've been ordered back to Aden!"

"The Japs surrendered!" Huw could hardly believe his ears. Every indication was that the Japanese would fight with suicidal ferocity to the last man. Surrendered? Too good to be true! "Are you sure?" he demanded.

"No doubt about it. Sparks says the airwaves are positively buzzing with messages. Seems the Yanks dropped some kind of super-bombs and wiped out several of their cities. Anyway, it looks as though it was enough to make them realise that, if they went on, there would be no home-land left for them to continue fighting for! With any luck, we'll be ordered back to Blighty."

The rest of that day was a confused blur for Huw. Eventually, the reality did sink in. It was over. He had survived. Whatever tedious days lay ahead before he could be de-mobbed and start to pick up the threads of civilian life, he did have a future, a future which was bound up with that of Zara.

Huw and his fellow diver-pilots were flown back via Athens and Rome in a Dakota, arriving at dawn at an RAF airfield south of Croydon. Orders were waiting for him to report that afternoon to Rear-Admiral Timpson in Whitehall. After being kept waiting for over an hour, he was ushered into Timpson's office. His heart missed a beat when he saw a subdued-looking Zara seated there. Timpson did not get up and Huw saluted and stood to attention.

"I understand," said the Rear-Admiral, "that in flagrant disobedience to orders, you have made contact with Miss Khan here."

"Yes, sir." Huw said as neutrally as he could. He had no desire to make matters worse by being truculent. Nor, on the other hand, was he prepared to be the slightest bit apologetic.

"I see. And what are your intentions now? Do you plan to continue this friendship?"

The older man's officious prying into what Huw regarded as his private life irked him, but he remained cool. "If that is what Miss Khan wishes, sir."

"You realise that this means that you should be put on a charge?"

"So be it", Huw replied, trying to stifle any emotion that might creep into his voice.

"And that this could also affect your long-term prospects in the Navy?"

So what? thought Huw. He had no long-term ambitions that did not include Zara. Anger was surging within him. Was this senior officer merely displeased that standing orders had been broken? Or was it the fact that a white officer under his command was pursuing a friendship, or possibly a romance, with a coloured woman? He decided to force the issue.

"Long-term prospects in the Navy are a secondary consideration for me, sir. I intend to ask Miss Khan to do me the honour of letting me become her husband just as soon as I am sufficiently settled to offer her a home."

A long silence followed. Zara shifted uneasily in her chair. Now I've really done it! thought Huw. The Rear-Admiral leaned forward over his desk and steepled his hands under his chin. Eventually he spoke. Turning to Zara, he asked. "And you? What have you to say for yourself?"

"If Lieutenant Morgan did propose to me, I should be delighted to accept!"

There was a further silence, broken at last by the senior officer, "Well, thank the Lord that some happiness may yet come out of the tragedy of this whole beastly war. I didn't bring you here so that I could act as a marriage broker, but I'm glad to be the first to congratulate you both!"

Chapter 18

The months following the end of the war were a strange sort of anti-climax. Huw's diving experience was greatly in demand as the tired and battered continent of Europe returned to some semblance of normality. There were mine-fields and under-water obstacles to be cleared. There were block-ships to be raised so that blockaded ports could be brought back into use. There was a seemingly unending amount of salvage work to be done, such had been the number of ships sent to the bottom by both sides in the years of conflict. However, Huw did not see the Navy as being his life-time's work. What he really wanted to do was to become a doctor. However, there seemed to be no possibility of that, especially as Zara and he were planning their wedding for the early part of 1946.

Zara was no longer required in the intelligence work she had been doing and was becoming increasingly frustrated at the series of mind-numbing routine clerical jobs she was given. The two were able to see quite a lot of each other. The rather stress-filled experience of each being introduced to the other's family passed off much more happily than they had expected. Zara had taught Huw to speak Urdu and Mr Khan was quite delighted that his future son-in-law was reasonably proficient in that language.

Just before Christmas, both received a letter from Rear-Admiral Timpson inviting them to dinner at his West End Club. With some trepidation they went, wondering what was in store for them. Considering the chronic food shortages that gripped the whole country, they fed well, talking over past experiences as they did so. When coffee had been served, it became obvious that the Rear-Admiral was about to come to the point of the whole evening.

"I understand you're getting married in March?" he asked.

"Yes, sir, the 23rd."

"And what are your plans thereafter, if I may ask?"

"I'll have to stay on in the Navy for the time-being, but in the long term, I would like to work in a hospital."

"A hospital! Why?"

"I used to do first-aid work before the war, sir. I used to dream about training as a doctor, but that was out of the question then and, I'm afraid, still is. However, I may get work as some kind of auxiliary."

"And you, Zara? What are your ambitions?" Timpson asked, turning to the hitherto silent half of his two guests.

"Even more unlikely dreams," she smiled. "I wanted to be a surgeon. A silly girlhood dream! The reality is that I'll continue in clerical work until we can afford to have a family."

The older man was silent for a couple of minutes. Then he started to speak about what had clearly been in his mind when he had asked them to dine with him that evening.

"That confirms what I had heard on the grape-vine about your hopes and dreams." He paused for a long minute, then went on, "I started this war with three sons. The first to go was killed at Dunkirk. The second was lost when the Hood was sunk by the Bismarck. The third was captured by the Japanese. I kept hoping he would be spared but I've just heard that he died of dysentery at a slave-labour camp building a railway in Burma." His eyes welled with unshed tears.

A profound silence followed. Neither of the two younger members of the group knew what to say and, wisely, they said nothing. Eventually, the older man recovered his composure.

"I want you two young people to do me a favour. I

had expected my boys to go to university and I was amply able to pay for their education. I want you two to let me fund your training as doctors. No! Don't interrupt." He waved his hand to silence them as both started to speak at once. "I wondered about having some kind of memorial built to my lads, but I can't think of a better way of honouring them than giving this country two highly trained and dedicated doctors. You will accept, won't you?"

The two were too flabbergasted to speak. They nodded mutely and Timpson went on.

"With this new National Health Service, there's going to be a terrific demand for doctors. I can pull strings and get you both out of the Navy's clutches and into medical school. Now, please tell me you'll do it!"

So they both became doctors. Huw went into general practice. Zara became an orthopaedic surgeon.

Chapter 19

The years that followed were years of hard work, yet very happy ones. The wedding was a very quiet affair, with post-war austerity and food-rationing making a lavish celebration impossible. Friends and family rallied round, each contributing food or sweet coupons, but even so, the reception was small and the food-supply meagre. None of this, however, affected the general happiness of the occasion.

The bride had baked and decorated the cake herself. It was a plain-looking single-tier affair with a wafer-thin layer of icing but it was the best she could do with the available ingredients. There were the usual photographs taken for the family album, but even the number of these was severely limited. The one that had to be included at all costs was the traditional cake-cutting ceremony. Huw stood awkwardly beside his bride, wishing things could have been different and that he could have made the occasion more worthy of her. Zara placed her hand over his on the knife as they posed.

She caught his eye, glanced down and moved the point of the knife so slightly that only Huw noticed. His eye followed hers and he suddenly realised that the strange decorations on the white icing were, in fact, Morse. The knife pointed to: PGRB QR1 SMFK

QR1! International code for 'Request permission to lie alongside.' Their eyes met. Their faces were lit up in the mutual sharing of the secret joke. The camera clicked, and for ever more friends and family commented on the radiant smiles of the bridal pair.

After that, Morse and the International Code became a secret language the two used when they wished to communicate with one another. At a cock-tail party or other similar function, this became a serious way of ensuring that each knew what the other was thinking. If, for instance, one, in ignorance, was starting to touch on a delicate subject, a flicker of the eye-lids could signal U - 'You are running into danger.' If that was insufficient, the signal would be JB -'There is a danger of explosion'. If Zara, as did happen from time to time, found herself monopolised by some intolerable bore, she would send NC -'I am in distress and require immediate assistance.'

As time went by, the use of these codes became an art-form and neither colleagues nor family twigged what was going on. Some remarked on the almost telepathic understanding of each other that the two had. A prudish older colleague was overheard saying, "Really, the way that woman flutters her eyes at her husband! You'd think they were newly-weds, not a middle-aged couple."

Others giggled at the way the two walked hand in hand, little guessing what, by means of subtle changes of hand pressure, was being silently said in Morse about them by the Morgans. If the company became too boring, one or other would signal SF1 - 'Are you ready to get under way?' and, like one soul in two bodies, they would both make their apologies and leave.

Their two sons arrived in the early fifties. One now lived in Vancouver, the other in Hong Kong. They had both come for the Golden Wedding celebrations, but there was no doubt that time and distance had loosened the close bonds of the family. They had been close when the boys were growing up. However, when one went to Cardiff to study law and the other to Cambridge to read physics, the drift apart began. It was about that time that Rear-Admiral Timpson, now retired, had introduced Commander Robertson to them. The worsening situation in Northern Ireland was causing serious anxiety in security circles and the need to gather information was acute. There were vacancies for medical people in Belfast. Would the Morgans be prepared to go there? In all fairness, Timpson had done nothing to pressure them in any way. It was Robertson who had made a convincing case for serving the cause of peace and reconciliation by frustrating the schemes of the gun-men and the bombers. So Zara went to work in a hospital in Belfast and Huw became a GP in a run-down Catholic area.

Neither of the Morgans allied themselves to either faction in the struggle that was making Northern Ireland a by-word for bitterness, brutality and bigotry. By being scrupulously fair in their treatment of all who came to them, they tended to be accepted by both sections of the community. It seemed to be assumed by patients and staff alike at the hospital that, because of her colour, Zara would be of some eastern faith. This was really ironical because first Zara, then Huw, developed in this period of their lives a genuine faith based, not on the traditions of either Catholics or Protestants, but on the Bible. This faith bore little or no resemblance to the unloving bigotry which was a fact of life in Ulster. Their beliefs much more closely resembled the teaching of a Christ who taught, "Love your enemy. If he is hungry, feed him. If he is thirsty, give him a drink." However, their shared faith was a quiet and private matter between them and their God. It contrasted sharply with the environment in which they now lived. Here, in the name of either Christianity, liberty, patriotism - or indeed, of all three, the most appalling atrocities were committed and applauded. In a world that was shrinking and in Europe, in particular, where countries were coming together in economic and political co-operation which was bringing unprecedented peace and prosperity, the attitudes current in Northern Ireland were a ridiculous anachronism. That is, to all except the Irish. It was about this time that the night-time call-outs for casualties of the troubles began.

The operation on McPhee was the first of many similar occasions when IRA men who had been wounded were patched up. The two doctors often wondered what would have happened to them had McPhee died. His remarkable recovery clearly raised their status in the eyes of his terrorist colleagues and they were frequently pressed into service. On these occasions, some conversation between the IRA men was in Gaelic and Huw was careful never to give the slightest indication that he understood a word. Most of what was said was in English and the terrorists once or twice, with apparent lack of discretion, talked about future attacks on the authorities that they had planned. Huw and Zara guessed that they were being tested and they took the risk of not passing on any of this to Commander Robertson. Huw and Zara did try to talk during one of these night-time emergency operations in Urdu, but were forcibly told that everything they said must be in English. So they were forced back more and more on Morse and the old war-time codes. There was a strange irony about discussing an IRA man during an operation by tapping a lancet on his skin!

There had been several very tense times. In 1976, there had been even more casualties to be attended to than usual. As luck would have it, some of these were so severely wounded that nothing could be done apart from pain control. More worrying, however, was the fact that many more patients, some with quite minor injuries, contracted secondary infections and died. This fact was no great surprise to the Morgans. The desperately primitive conditions under which they were working should make a successful recovery very much the exception rather than the rule. Whether the terrorists would see things that way was not clear. The unexpectedly long run of successful outcomes in the earlier operations perhaps raised the two doctors to a pinnacle of repute that they simply could not live up to. Now there seemed to be an unparalleled series of disasters. Then, just when they were wondering if the next death on the operating table would result in their own deaths, their luck seemed just as unaccountably to change. The operating conditions were as bad as ever, but almost all their patients survived. So the clandestine operating theatres continued to function.

Meanwhile, Huw's surgery was a perfect information exchange and several 'patients' who were working for the government under cover, made frequent visits and left clutching prescription forms. Once the doctors were satisfied that they had been accepted, if not as allies by the IRA, at least as benevolent neutrals in the conflict, it became possible to pass on valuable snippets of information to Commander Robertson's organisation. The results were sometimes disappointing, but at other times very gratifying as the authorities managed to frustrate the terrorists and to make arrests. This went on until one evening in 1979. The doctors had been out at a function one evening and were driving home. Their car was stopped at an Army road-block and they were ordered out. Under armed guard, they were rushed to the nearest police station. There, to their surprise, was Commander Robertson.

"I do apologise for all the drama. We've been reliably informed that the Ulster Defence Association have discovered that you've been helping wounded IRA men and that they're going to blow up your house as soon as you get home. Ironical, isn't it! There are few who've done more than you two to frustrate the IRA, and the Protestants want to kill you! They'll hear that you've been pulled in for questioning, so I don't think your house will be hit tonight. However, it'll only be a stay of execution. I think we've got to accept that the good work you've been doing must come to a close."

For most of the rest of that night they discussed tactics. Decisions were made with the result that, the very next day, Huw contacted the press and issued a statement that Zara and he were not prepared to go on working in a city where they were detained half the night by an officious police force. All they had sought to do was to serve the divided people of Ireland without religious discrimination of any sort. Their treatment at the hands of the authorities was a disgrace and the two doctors were retiring forthwith and returning to England.

Chapter 20

The ice-house at Port Appin, 1996

The door of the ice-house was swung open and the two Irishmen entered. Zara pretended to still be unconscious as one bent over her and made a superficial check on her bonds. The other poked Huw with his foot and said in Gaelic.

"Both still alive. More's the pity! Must be a pair of tough old birds! Chuck her in the van. I'll bring the old fellow. We'd better get away from here before anyone misses them."

"I don't think we need worry much. I chucked the old dear's hand-bag and phone in the water. With any luck, they'll be found and it will be assumed that they were cut off by the tide and drowned."

Zara immediately recognised McPhee's voice even though nearly twenty years had gone by since she was last in his company. The crucial question now was would he recognise her? If he did, then their fate was definitely sealed. If he did not, there was perhaps a ghost of a chance that the two would be dumped in some out of the way spot whilst the terrorists went about their unlawful business. She then rebuked herself for being silly enough to entertain such a hope.

"Couldn't we just dump them in the water as well? It'll save having to take them with us?"

"Could've done if you hadn't banged their heads so hard. Now, if they were found promptly, even a country copper would spot the injuries and the marks of the ropes. Then there would be an immediate murder hunt. No! We'll take them well away from here and make sure their bodies'll not be found until long after we've done our job and are safely back in Ireland."

So saying, the two men hoisted Zara and Huw on to their shoulders and dumped them roughly into the back of a waiting van. A faint smell of petrol permeated the vehicle. The two windows in the rear door had been rendered opaque by the liberal application of paint on the inside. At the front, behind the driver's and passenger's seats, a crude curtain hung, concealing the contents of the van from prying eyes. The result was that the cargo space of the van was almost completely dark.

Huw slipped the lashings on his hands and sat up. He tried the rear doors of the van, but was not at all surprised to find them securely locked. In addition to the standard Transit lock, there seemed to be a hasp and padlock arrangement on the outside. He had been thrown on top of the long flat boxes that he had assumed contained guns. A quick examination showed that the boxes were extremely strongly made. The lids were nailed down and then they had been painted with some kind of rubbery stuff, no doubt to make them water-tight. Without a crow-bar or a jemmy there was no hope of opening them. The rest of the space in front of them was piled to within two feet of the ceiling with plastic containers. Huw sniffed round the lid of one and concluded it contained petrol. At this point, the van engine burst into life. The unmistakable sound and

vibration of a diesel engine confirmed that the petrol smell was from the cargo, not the fuel tank of the van. He explored further. There was another kind of container and with some difficulty he eased a lid off. This was packed with a greyish powder, the stuff he had assumed was the IRA home-made explosive.

Huw wriggled to where he could touch Zara and started tapping out a message to her.

"You OK? This is a massive car-bomb. Explosives and petrol. Imagine this lot going off in a crowded street!"

"What to do? Any ideas?" Was the terse Morse reply.

At this point, the van reached what was obviously a main road and was soon bowling along at a good speed. With the increase in speed, the noise-level rose and Huw felt safe enough to speak without the risk of being overheard.

"I'm sorry I got you into this and I can't see any way out. We'd better assume we've only got an hour at the most. My guess is that they'll head inland and take some remote back-road. Then they'll kill us at some suitably lonely spot before heading south again on the main roads. I'm sorry to be so pessimistic, but we might as well face reality."

"I'm sure you're right. If we can't get out, we can

at least make sure this lot doesn't reach London."

She slipped her bonds and pulled Huw's lighter out of her pocket. Huw looked at her with a mix of horror and admiration.

Zara saw the look on his face. "What was it you said back in the hotel? Your beloved Tennyson? 'Something ere the end, some work of noble note may yet be done!' Well! This is it!"

"You mean that, don't you?" said Huw slowly, a deep awe in his voice.

"The alternative is to humbly wait for them to kill us. We'll be dead and who knows how many others will die in London. The chance of a peace settlement will go and the slaughter continue in Ireland into the indefinite future. I don't think we've much choice."

"I suppose you're right."

"You know I am," replied Zara with a determined look on her face. "Let's get the lids off as many of these petrol cans as we can. Leave them loose on top so that our friends up front don't notice the smell. At the critical moment, we'll tip a few over and strike a light."

Quickly and silently they got to work. When all the reachable cans had had their lids removed, the old couple sat down and held hands. There was nothing much left to be said, only the sharing of a last few loving moments together.

Chapter 21

A series of burglaries at remote country houses in the Oban district had been plaguing the local police. The stolen goods were turning up in Edinburgh and Glasgow and the assumption was that the raids were the work of a gang from the Lowlands. During that particular night, a house had been raided but this time there was a silent alarm which alerted the police. The location of the house was, however, so far from the nearest police station that the thieves had escaped. Road-blocks were quickly set up on route every leading south. This included the narrow back road that McPhee's Transit van was now on.

The two policemen had chosen the spot for their road-block well. Although the flashing light on their car gave adequate warning, the road coming from the north was hemmed in on both sides by substantial stone walls and even a small car could not have made a quick three-point turn and head north again. The police car was drawn up beside the road at the only part where it widened slightly because of the presence of a small loch on the east side. All the cars to use the road so far that morning were those of local people. The two constables did their work diligently, however, and even the well-known local doctor had had to open his car boot.

As the Transit approached the block, PC Grainger was checking the boot of an old Cavalier, whilst PC Bell stood by, watching the Transit as it slowed down behind a Volkswagen van. As Grainger waved on the Cavalier, Bell spoke to the driver of the Volkswagen.

In the Transit, McPhee and his companion conferred. "There's no way we can turn back. We'll just have to take the pair of them out. Get the guns ready."

"What about that van in front?"

"We'll let it go, stall the coppers for long enough to let it out of ear-shot, then we'll blow them away. We'll drag their bodies out of sight and switch off the light on their car. With any luck it'll be an hour or more before the alarm is raised. By then we'll be well away"

The two sat, cradling their automatic pistols on their knees. As the police slammed the door of the Volkswagen shut, McPhee glanced in the rear-view mirror and looked back up the road.

"Blast!" he said. "Another car coming. We'll just have to take them out too. Get the coppers first and then belt round the back before the lot behind realise what is happening. What the blazes is that?"

'That' was Huw and Zara energetically pulling over the petrol containers in the back of the van. McPhee hauled at the curtain and it came away in his hand. He took in the scene at a glance. As he raised his gun, Zara smiled at him. Instantly he recognised her and hesitated. Zara held up the lighter and flicked the lever.

PC Grainger caught the full blast of the explosion. His hair and his clothes alight, he sailed gracefully through the air and splashed down in the loch in a cloud of steam. That saved his life, although he was

very badly injured. PC Bell was luckier. He had walked back to the front of the Volkswagen to tell the driver he was free to go. The van stood between him and the Transit, so he was not caught in the fire-ball. He was, however, knocked to the ground as the blast lifted the Volkswagen and threw it bodily forward about eight feet. Instinctively, he thought about the fire-extinguisher in the police car and then immediately forgot it. He might as well try to put the fire out by spitting on it. A fully equipped fire-engine would find this blaze difficult to quell. The searing heat forced him back, dragging the driver of the already smouldering Volkswagen with him. Appalled, he watched as the raging flames surged out to envelop and cremate the two men who had been blown partially through the windscreen and whose bodies hung grotesquely out of the front of the Transit. Above the roar of the inferno came the crackle of exploding ammunition.

Still stunned, Bell plunged into the loch to rescue his colleague who had escaped death by fire only to be in danger of drowning. Staggering ashore dragging the prostrate form of his fellow policeman with him, Bell shouted instructions to the shell-shocked Volkswagen driver to call for help on the police car radio. He then set about giving his colleague mouth-to-mouth resuscitation.

Chapter 22

The news of the explosion dominated the news for the next several days. The national papers carried only a short paragraph about the search for the two elderly doctors who were missing from their hotel in Oban. A helicopter had scoured the beaches but, apart from a few personal possessions identified as belonging to the missing couple, it found nothing. The presence of their car parked near Port Appin tended to confirm the sad assumption that the two had been caught by the rising tide.

Three months later, Clifford and David Morgan, the one from Hong Kong and the other from Vancouver, visited Oban. There had been, as seemed appropriate, a memorial service, but the attendance was thin. As with many who survive into their seventies and eighties, the two had outlived most of their friends and colleagues and none was left to speak of their achievements. The two brothers sat in the hotel in shared silence on their last night. The television in the back-ground was on but they were not listening.

The news-caster droned on, "The Prime Minister today said that what was now being called 'The Downing Street Agreement' offered the best chance for a generation of a new start and a stable peace in Northern Ireland. He urged all parties to exercise restraint and to work to make the agreement a success..........Police in the Highlands are now conceding that they will probably never know the identity of the two older IRA members who were killed in the 'own-goal' explosion of their Transit van near the Pass of Brander. The forensic evidence suggests that these two must have been veterans of the early days of the troubles but IRA sources are refusing to identify them......."

The Morgan brothers left Scotland next morning. They had arranged for a memorial bench to be placed overlooking the firth where their parents were presumed to have perished. On it was to be a plaque recording the dead couple's names. They had thought of putting as a text the passage from the Bible that the vicar had quoted at the memorial service.

"In life, they were loved and gracious and, in death, they were not parted."

It was, after all, very appropriate. However, eventually they settled for an extract from Tennyson's Ulysses:

'One equal temper of heroic hearts,
made weak by time and fate, but strong in will,

to strive, to seek, to find, and not to yield'

Their father was very fond of quoting Tennyson. He would have liked that.